REBELLIOUS SECRETS

SECRETS OF THE HEART SERIES - BOOK 3

ELIZABETH ROSE

ROSESCRIBE MEDIA INC.

Cover created by Elizabeth Rose Krejcik
Edited by Scott Moreland

ISBN: 9781731233509

TO MY READERS

Secrets of the Heart is a series about the daughters of the bastard triplets from the *Legendary Bastards of the Crown Series.* If you'd like to read about Rowen, Rook, and Reed who are the girls' fathers, or about the bastard triplets' sisters in the *Seasons of Fortitude Series* I have listed the books in each series for you.

Legendary Bastards of the Crown:
    Destiny's Kiss – Series Prequel
    Restless Sea Lord – Book 1
    Ruthless Knight – Book 2
    Reckless Highlander – Book 3

Seasons of Fortitude Series:
    Highland Spring – Book 1
    Summer's Reign – Book 2
    Autumn's Touch – Book 3
    Winter's Flame – Book 4

Secrets of the Heart Series:

   Highland Secrets – Book 1

   Seductive Secrets – Book 2

   Rebellious Secrets – Book 3

   Forgotten Secrets – Book 4

Enjoy!

                   Elizabeth Rose

CHAPTER 1

*M*aira Douglas swore to never eavesdrop again after what she'd just heard.

Standing in the shadows of the great hall of Castle Rothbury, Maira listened to her father, Rowen of Whitehaven, talking to her guardian, Lord Walter Beaufort of Rothbury, Earl of Northumberland. Having heard her name mentioned at the wedding of her cousin, Willow, she wandered over to learn more.

"Your daughter is twenty years of age now," the earl told Rowen. "I have mentored her as well as your nieces for many years, as you know."

"Aye, Earl. And I am ever so grateful. However, remember, it was by the king's dying wish that you do so," Maira's father reminded the man.

"I'm sure King Edward never meant for the girls to stay with me this long!"

Rowen took a swig of ale from his tankard and slowly nodded. "Fia and Willow are no longer under your guardianship, so I can only imagine you want to be relieved of your commitment where my daughter, Maira, and my niece, Morag, are concerned."

"It's not that, Whitehaven," grumbled the earl, not sounding at all convincing.

"It's just that I have been summoned to King Richard's side and will be leaving on the morrow to campaign for him in France. I am not sure when I'll return."

"Then I'll take the girls with me, back to Whitehaven," offered Rowen.

"Nay. Face it, Rowen. You need to betroth your daughter. No man is going to want a woman well in her prime to bear his heirs. Especially with the way that one acts like a man!"

"Prime?" Maira whispered to herself. "I'm not that old! And I do not act like a man."

"Maira, I heard what the earl and yer faither said." Her meddlesome cousin, Morag, appeared right behind her. The girl seemed to be everywhere and always had her nose in everyone's business. "Ye ken he's right. Ye need to marry like Fia and Willow. Ye are next in line."

"I don't want to marry. Ever." Maira ran her hand over the hilt of her dagger hanging from her belt. Her skill with weapons was better than a lot of the new recruits for squires. She was proud of it. "I want to be a warrior, just like my father."

"Maira, come here," her father called out, nodding toward her.

She didn't want to go to him, but had no choice. This wasn't going to be a pleasant conversation.

"Aye, Father?" She faked a smile. "Are you enjoying Willow's wedding celebration?"

Rowen looked over to his two brothers, Rook and Reed who were arm wrestling each other with a crowd of people looking over their shoulders. The wedding celebration had lasted almost a sennight now. The two brothers had once again drunk too much and were trying to outdo each other in any way possible.

"I'm sure I'm not enjoying the celebration as much as those two fools." Rowen shook his head, scoffing at them. Out of the triplet brothers, Rowen had always been the voice of reason. Each of the men had a personality of their own. "Rook, Reed, stop causing a scene," he called out.

"No' until I show the fool that Scots are stronger than Sassenachs," Reed shouted back. He was the redhead of the three and lived in Scotland, always talking, dressing and acting like a Scot since the boys had grown up in Scotland being raised by Ross Douglas.

"Maira, I have something to tell you," said Rowen, looking as nervous as Maira felt.

"What is it, Father?"

"Ye ken what it is," said Morag, pushing her way into the conversation. "He's betrothin' ye, just like we heard him say."

"You were eavesdropping." Rowen flashed Maira a disappointed look.

"Mayhap I was, but now I wish I hadn't. Father, I don't want to be betrothed to anyone," Maira told him, never afraid to stand up for what she believed.

"The earl is leaving to campaign in France for Richard."

"Then can't I come home with you?" asked Maira hopefully. "I miss Mother and haven't seen her in quite some time."

"And, mayhap, I can go home to Scotland," added Morag excitedly.

Rowen and the earl exchanged glances. Then Rowen cleared his throat and continued. "Maira, I've already made plans for you. The earl believes it would be beneficial for me to make an alliance with the High Sheriff of Durham."

"Alliance?" asked Maira. "You mean you want me to marry this man."

"Sir Gregory Arundell of Durham holds a high position, not to mention he is rich," said the earl, Lord Beaufort, as if that would matter to her. "You would be wise to consider the marriage, Maira."

"Father, nay," she protested. "If I must remind you, the king granted me permission on his deathbed to agree or disagree to any betrothal."

"That's right, he did," agreed Morag. "Fia told me so."

"I am well aware of what King Edward said. I was there," said Rowen with a stiff upper lip. "Maira, you will leave for Durham Castle on the morrow to meet Sir Gregory. After a month of living there, you will get to know him. Then, I'm sure you'll see that he is a good choice for you."

"A month?" spat Maira. "You might as well put me in the dungeon right now because, to me, that is a horrible punishment. Why can't I just come home with you, Father?"

"It's for the best," the earl told her. "Give yourself some time to know the man, like your father mentioned. I'm sure you will agree with us in the end."

"Do you like this High Sheriff, Father?" asked Maira.

"I have never met the man," Rowen admitted. "But I am taking the earl's word for it, as I trust his judgment. He has never steered us wrong before."

"I never met him either," said the earl. "But I asked the Bishop of Durham about the man and he had naught but good things to say. I'll take the holy man's word for it."

"I don't want to go," Maira said, trying one last time to change her father's mind. "I'll be all alone and won't know anyone there. Father, you can't mean to put me in such a position. You don't want me to be lonely, do you?"

"Well, nay, I wouldn't want that," her father mumbled, looking at the ground.

"She can take Morag along with her," said the earl, making Maira want to muffle the man.

Rowen's head jerked up and he looked at the girls. "Aye, that's a fine idea. Then you won't feel lonely, Maira, since you'll have your cousin along with you. I'll tell Reed right away that his daughter will be going to Durham, too." Rowen glanced over his shoulder. "That is, if the fool ever stops with the arm wrestling."

"Beat ye!" cried out Reed, jumping up from the stool and slamming his empty tankard down on the table. He moved so fast that the bench toppled over, taking two men with it. Half the crowd cheered and the other half booed. "Now, someone bring me some more Mountain Magic because I've got some celebratin' to do."

"My da is drinkin' Mountain Magic?" asked Morag with a roll of her eyes. "That's no' guid. When he's well in his cups, there is no talkin' any sense into him." Morag flipped her long, blond braid over her shoulder and crossed her arms in front of her, letting out a deep sigh. "I guess I'm comin' with ye, Maira. So we might as well make the best of it."

"Father, please don't make me do this," begged Maira, trying once again to change her father's decision. "You know how miserable I'll be. Besides, I'm not going to agree to the marriage so it's just a waste of everyone's time."

"I don't know," said her father, looking over to the earl as if he might change his mind. Maira was Rowen's only daughter and often she could convince him to agree to what she wanted. The only trouble was that the earl held more influence over her father than she did.

"It's a smart move, Whitehaven, so don't make a decision you'll regret later," warned the earl. "You know as well as I that you could use the alliance."

Maira's father looked back at her, keeping his jaw tight. He took one more swig of ale, smacking his lips together before he spoke. "Two weeks instead of a month, Maira," he answered in finality. "But you are going to Durham Castle, like it or not. And I want you to leave behind your weapons and act like a lady while you're there. No sense scaring off the man before he gets to know you. And that is exactly what will happen when he sees the way you act."

"Leave behind my weapons?" The thought was appalling to Maira. What was her father saying? He knew how much practicing with her sword and daggers meant to her. "I can't do that. You are the one who gave the weapons to me in the first place. How can you order me not to use them?"

Rowen nodded and looked as if he felt bad about the deal. "All right, then. You can take them with you, but I want them locked away at all times, do you understand? You are not to be seen with your sword on your back or your daggers attached to your waist belt. No bow and arrows either."

"This isn't fair!" she shouted, feeling like she was being sentenced for no reason at all.

"Rowen, get over here," called out Maira's Uncle Rook. "Reed is cheating. We need you to be the judge."

"I wish Mother was here, because she would listen to me," said Maira, feeling like crying. But she wouldn't cry because that would make her look weak. Maira was known as the strongest of all the girl cousins in her family and she liked that reputation.

"Your mother has other things taking her concern right now," Rowen told her. "Little Michael has been ill lately, and also acting up again. So I don't want you sending missives about this to Whitehaven because you will only worry her. Now, go get packed. You and Morag will leave for Durham in the morning." He turned and walked away with the earl, heading toward the crowd. The conversation was over and his decision was final. There was nothing more Maira could do.

"Morag, would you really come with me to Durham?" Maira asked her cousin.

"It doesna seem as if I have a choice. But I dinna mind," said Morag. "Since she's married, Fia is takin' all the attention with the new bairn so no one will even notice if I'm there or no'. I sometimes think that I've been forgotten."

"Then go get Fia and Willow and meet me in the secret garden," Maira told her. The families were still there cele-brating Willow's wedding but they would be leaving soon. Maira turned and started across the great hall.

"Do ye mean Imanie's garden?" asked Morag, running after her.

"Of course I mean Imanie's garden. Do you know another secret garden? Now, go. Tell them this is important and to come alone. I need to talk to them anon."

"All right," said Morag, stopping in her tracks.

7

Maira called over her shoulder. "And whatever you do, don't bring Branton along." The page that longed to be a squire was starting to be just as troublesome as Morag lately. He already knew too many of the girls' secrets. Maira decided that even though she liked to spar with him, she should start to distance herself from him if possible.

She made her way to the stable and mounted her horse, making her way to the secret garden. Chosen by the late Queen Philippa, Maira, as well as her cousins, Willow and Fia, were members of a secret group of strong women called the Followers of the Secret Heart. Morag had meddled her way into the group as a member before their old mentor, Imanie, dropped dead from a bad heart.

Maira wore her crown today since she and her cousins were allowed to wear the late queen's jeweled crowns during important celebrations and gatherings. Maira's headpiece was a thin gold band loaded down with sparkling rubies and yellow amber stones. Fia had the bulkiest crown, and Willow's was a good size as well. But Maira liked hers because it was thinner and lighter and wouldn't weigh her down if she had to protect herself and use her sword to fight.

With her sword strapped to her back and her daggers at her side, Maira rode quickly through the woods to the edge of the earl's land. The secret garden was found where his land and the king's lands met. Within it was a little cottage made from wattle and daub where their mentor, Imanie, used to live.

As soon as Maira approached the half-hidden gate, she swung her legs over the side of her steed and dismounted. Quickly scanning her surroundings, she checked to make sure she hadn't been followed. Since this garden was in the royal forest, no one dared to bother it. And for the most part, it was safe.

Maira pushed open the gate and led her horse inside. On the far side of the enclosed space was Imanie's cottage as well as a single covered stable that had, at one time, housed her horse. On the other side of the house was a shed that held gardening tools of all kinds. When she had first seen this garden, it had looked like the abode of a fairy. It seemed so magical and was well kept. It had beautiful blooming flowers and a variety of healthy vegetables. But since Imanie's death, the girls had not tended to the grounds like they probably should have. It was only recently that Willow and her husband's sister, Hazel, had started caring for the garden again.

She tied her horse to a tree and headed toward the house. The weeds were nearly as tall as her. It was like walking through the forest once again. Maira wasn't as tall as Willow or Fia, but she made up for it in strength and determination. Each of the girls had a special skill and was mentored by Imanie to use their talents wisely. It was the purpose of this group to make important changes but also, in the process, to make men think those choices or happenings were because of them. After all, women were not respected nor were they allowed to have choices. Her father proved that by making her agree to live with a man who she had no intention of marrying.

"I don't want to go," she said, kicking at a stone. The whinny of a horse caught her attention and she stopped in her tracks. The sound didn't come from the gate, so she knew it wasn't her cousins. Nay, this noise came from inside the stable.

In one motion, she drew the sword from her back and held it steady with two hands, letting the tip of the blade lead her way to the stable.

"Who goes there?" she called out, ready to fight if need be.

As she approached, a man stepped out into the clearing holding out a sword aimed toward her as well. He was tall and wore a cloak over a dark green tunic and brown breeches. His hood was up and his face remained hidden in shadow.

"Put down the sword before you're hurt," directed the man in a low voice.

"Who are you?" she asked curiously and cautiously. "And what are you doing here?" She gripped the hilt of her sword tighter.

Her eyes settled on a burlap bag flung over the man's shoulder. Sticking out of the top of the bag she noticed what looked like the iron poker from the hearth from Imanie's cottage.

"I'm just passing through, so there's no need for alarm," he told her. "Now turn around and get on your horse and forget you ever saw me."

"Forget I ever saw you?" she asked, wondering if this man thought she was a fool. "Nay, I will do naught of the sort. You're stealing!" she spat. "You are a thief, and I am not about to turn away and let you leave here with things that don't belong to you."

"And what are you going to do about it?" he asked with a chuckle. "Fight me with that mighty sword? I'm surprised you can even hold the bloody thing."

"Then you'll be surprised by this as well." Maira lunged forward, swiping her sword at the man.

Startled, he stepped back quickly. The tip of his sword

lowered in the process. From his sudden motion, the bag fell from his shoulder. Imanie's possessions spilled out over the ground. "Your blade ripped my tunic," the man said in shock. His hand fingered the cloth over his chest.

"Put down your sword and get on your horse and ride away," she repeated his warning back to him. "Do it, or the next move I make will be my blade ripping through your flesh instead."

"Egads, what's the matter with you, wench?" growled the man. "Don't you know I could kill you right where you stand before you even have a chance to strike again?"

"We'll see about that!" She shot forward and her sword clashed with his. When he moved, the hood fell from his head, enabling her to see his handsome face. He had sun-kissed golden skin. That told her he lived in the elements, or spent a goodly amount of time outdoors. And by the simple clothes he wore that blended in with the earth, she realized he must be a peasant. However, his fighting skills were as strong as those of a nobleman. Plus, he owned a sword. This made her very confused.

"I highly doubt a common thief could best me where my fighting skills are concerned," she told him. "I have learned from the best." She lunged forward and he parried.

"I must admit, I've never seen the likes of this," said the man. "Tell me, how does a wench know how to handle a weapon? Or for that matter, how does such a little thing like you even hold up a heavy sword at all?" His sudden interest in her felt good. She liked to be noticed for her strengths instead of scoffed at because of them. Especially from a man.

"Not that I need to tell you anything, but my sword is lightweight and is made especially for a lady," she bragged, continuing to spar with the man, "And I'm not a wench! I am Lady Maira Douglas," she answered proudly. "My father is the legendary Rowen the Restless. I'm sure you've heard of him."

"The pirate?" The man's brows arched. "Ah, that is why you can fight like a cutthroat."

"My father is no longer a pirate, and I don't fight like a cutthroat!" She didn't like this man's assumptions. It only angered her more than she already was. In one motion, she shot forward with her sword leading the way. But once again, the man agilely stepped aside. He was quick on his feet. Maira almost fell trying to stop abruptly. She spun around to see the stranger smiling as if he were amused.

"If I'm not mistaken, your father is a bastard of the late King Edward," he said.

"That's right." She raised her chin and looked at him down her nose. Whoever he was, he needed to respect her. "My father is a nobleman, so you'd better stop calling him a bastard," she said through gritted teeth. "He is a lord and very respected by his people. He is not a common thief like you."

"Really?" His sword pushed hers to the side. "Then correct me if I'm wrong, but wasn't your father as well as his brothers once referred to as the Demon Thief? They stole from their own father – the king! If that's not thievery, I don't know what is."

Maira flinched inwardly. She'd been hoping the man didn't know about all that. He must have heard it somewhere. It was hard to scare or impress him with her words when he already knew all about her family secrets.

"What's your point?" she asked the stranger. Her sword clashed with his once again.

"Why do you fight like a man when you are naught but a woman?" he rallied.

"I don't like you using the word naught," she spat. Her fury rose. "I am going to turn you in to the earl for theft. He'll have you thrown in the dungeon."

He stepped back, pulling the tip of his blade away from her. Then he chuckled. "This isn't the earl's land so he has no authority to do anything to me."

"Then I'll tell my cousin, King Richard, since it's his land. He'll have your head for trespassing and stealing from a dead woman's cottage."

"Whose place is this?" he asked with a nod of his head toward the house and garden.

"That's none of your concern." Once again she shot forward. His movements were graceful as if he were doing a dance. He spun around and when he faced her once again, he made a wide swoop, managing to disarm her. Her sword was knocked from her grip and clamored to the ground. Then his foot shot out and he swept her off her feet. Maira landed with a thud on her back with the air knocked from her lungs. When she reached for her dagger, the tip of his sword under her chin kept her from moving further.

"I wouldn't if I were you," he warned her.

"Please, don't kill me," she begged, not wanting to die this way. Had she been too bold to go up against a man in a real battle?

"I don't kill ladies." His proffered hand shot out and he waited. His steel gray eyes met hers and their gazes interlocked. All thoughts of kicking him in the groin, biting him, or pulling another blade on him, fled her mind when she saw the sweep of his perusal down her body and then back up, settling on her mouth. "Lady Maira," he said, the deep timbre of his voice rattling in her chest. It wasn't often she encountered such a handsome – and dangerous man with her name upon his tongue. "You look so small and frail, yet you have the tenacity of a wild boar protecting her young."

"Wild boar?" Her eyes shot upward and she narrowed them. "I don't like being compared to such an animal."

"Well then, let me rephrase that." Without waiting for her to take his hand, he reached out and pulled her to a standing position. His hand lingered and she felt the warmth of his palm in hers. It was intimate, exciting, and dangerous. She'd never felt this way about any man before. "You look like a queen with that crown on your head. And you possess the confidence of a ruler as well. However, your fierce demeanor, being a woman and all, really intrigues me." He released her hand, reaching for her crown. His fingers skimmed over the jewels and, for a moment, she thought he was going to steal it from her.

Not wanting to wait for that to happen, she pushed him away and drew her dagger, pointing it at him. "Don't touch my crown. You can't have it," she spat.

He smiled again, sighed, and then used his foot to flip her sword up from the ground. He caught it in one hand with his sword still clutched in the other. "If you insist on challenging me, then let's at least make it a fair fight, shall we?" He handed her sword to her, hilt first.

Her eyes darted down to the sword and then back up to his face. Her heartbeat sped up. What was he doing? She waved her dagger in the air in front of him. "This is a trick, I know it is."

"A trick?" The thought seemed to amuse him.

"You want me to reach for my sword so you can run your blade through my heart when I do."

"I assure you, I would never do that, my lady. Now, please, retrieve your sword."

Cautiously, and keeping her eyes on the thief, Maira reached out for her sword. When she did, he knocked the dagger from her hand and pulled her close to him. She landed hard up against his chest, trapped in his strong arms.

"I knew you'd trick me! Let me go," she shouted.

"I only wanted for you to realize how dangerous it is for a lady to be wielding a sword. No matter how well trained you are, you still will never be a match for any man's strength." His gaze dropped to her mouth. Her eyes focused on his lips as well. Then she became confused. For a moment, when he leaned closer to her, all she could think about was kissing him. Her eyes closed and her head fell back as she anticipated the sensuous, yet strong lips of this stranger pressed up against hers. It might have happened, but Morag interrupted as usual.

"Maira? What are ye doin'?" came Morag's voice from the gate as she rode her horse inside the secret garden. Maira's eyes sprang open. She kneed the man in the groin to release his hold on her. He let out a groan and stepped away.

"You are a feisty sprite, Lady Maira. For some reason, that excites me. But now, if you'll excuse me, I'll be on my way." He handed her sword back to her and turned to leave.

"Wait!" she called out, following him to his horse. "You are not taking Imanie's things."

"They're going to go to good use," he said, grabbing the satchel and mounting his horse. "Besides, you told me the woman was dead, so what does it matter?"

"You are starting to sound like my cousin, Willow," she retorted. "Now, give those things back to me, you thief."

"Nay, I won't. You'd be best off to go back to the castle, now, where you belong. Do some embroidery or play your harp, my lady. Because behind a blade is no place for any woman to be."

"How dare you talk to me that way! You don't even know me."

He adjusted the bag on his shoulder and turned his horse to face her. "I know that you need to go back to the castle where there are men to protect you from people like me."

"I don't need a man. I can protect myself."

"Can you, now? I suppose that was what you were doing with your eyes closed and your head tilted back, waiting for a kiss?" He nodded, looking smug as if he had proven his point. Then he took off toward the gate, managing to infuriate her even more by leaving in the middle of this conversation.

"I let you do that," she called out after him. "I could have stopped you if I had so wanted."

"Maira, who was that?" asked Willow, looking over her shoulder as the man left the garden. Morag led the way and Fia brought up the rear as they rode in a single line.

"I'd say by the looks of that sack of Imanie's things over his shoulder that he's a thief." Fia was the cousin who could read people. She was also very observant and had the ability to tell by one's actions or words things that others could not see.

"He was handsome," said Willow, always liking the men.

"Ye are married now, Cousin," said Morag. "Stop lookin' at the men. Ye have one! Leave them for Maira and me."

"I can still look but, honestly, I only have eyes for Conrad,"

Willow assured her with a dreamy look upon her face. "I rather like being married."

"Don't leave them for me, because I'm not interested," said Maira. "And Willow, you've only been married for a sennight. We'll see if your eye starts to wander and if your opinion changes any time soon."

"It won't! I assure you. I've reformed from flirting with men," Willow said with a smug nod. "I might still have to use my powers of persuasion on occasion since it is my duty as a member of the Followers of the Secret Heart. But if I do, it'll only be a job and not for pleasure."

"Well, don't waste your skill on that man," Maira told her, nodding toward the gate. "He is a man that none of us will ever want." She reached over her shoulder and slid her sword into the leather scabbard that was attached with a harness to her back.

"Why would ye say that?" asked Morag, always wanting to know more.

"Because, like Fia said, he is a thief." Maira walked over and rubbed the nose of her horse.

"Then perhaps we should go after him," suggested Fia.

"Aye, we need to tell the earl," added Willow.

"Don't bother." Maira shook her head "He's not important. He's naught but a petty thief in the night, stealing items from a dead woman. His actions here were stealing from the king, not the earl, since the secret garden is in the king's royal forest. The earl cannot do a thing about it. Now, the reason I called you all here was because I'm sure you heard from Morag by now that my father has betrothed me."

"I think that thief liked you," said Willow, looking over to the gate where the stranger had already disappeared. Her

17

thoughts focused on him instead of Maira. "You seemed to like him as well."

"I agree," answered Fia.

"We fought, and I kneed him in the groin," Maira pointed out. "I hardly think there was anything but animosity between us."

"Nay, that's no' true," said Fia with a shake of her head. "I could tell by both his and yer body actions that there was more to it than that."

Maira cringed inwardly. Sometimes, her cousin Fia's natural skill of being able to read people was invading. Maira didn't like anyone peering into her mind. It was hard to keep a secret from Fia.

"When we entered the garden, it looked like you two were going to kiss," Willow pointed out. "I could see your head tilted back and your eyes closed. And he had his hand on your chin."

Dang, the seductive cousin of the bunch would have spotted that a league away.

"Stop it, all of you," said Maira, feeling very uncomfortable about this whole situation. How can you say those things? That man told me to go back to the castle where the men could protect me. He even told me to embroider and play a harp and to give up swinging a blade! Can you believe that?"

"I canna," said Morag making a face. "After all, I dinna think ye even ken what to do with a needle, or a harp." She chuckled. "It's no' like ye've ever tried either of those things."

"Morag," said Maira, glaring at her. "Hold your whee as the Scots would say."

Morag rolled her eyes and shook her head. "At least get it right, dear cousin. It's haud yer wheesht."

"Whatever it is, it doesn't matter." Maira tired of talking of the stranger. "That man's opinion of how a lady should act is the way most men think. It's disgusting."

"He's right that a lady shouldn't be acting like a man," said Willow, fussing with her hair. She was too feminine at times and the exact opposite of Maira.

Fia spoke up next. "Remember, Maira, ye need to let men think that way. I hope ye didna do anythin' to make him suspicious."

"Nay." Maira looked down and played with the reins in her grip. "Not really."

"Maira, ye didna use yer weapons around him, did ye?" asked Fia. "We are supposed to keep our skills a secret and no' alert anyone by usin' them openly."

"Fia, ever since you got married and had a baby you worry like an old hen," snapped Maira. "I may have used my sword but it was only to protect myself, I assure you."

"It didn't look to me like you were in any danger from him," said Willow.

"Aye," agree Morag. "Ye two were standin' very close, like lovers."

"Lovers?" This interested Willow. "Maira, you almost had me believing that you didn't like men. I guess it was all an act after all. I knew it!" Willow thrust her chin in the air and pushed back a lock of her long, ebony hair.

"Ye'd better stop kissin' the men since ye are leavin' on the morrow to get married," added the meddlesome Morag.

"I wasn't kissing him and I'm not marrying anyone, no matter what my father and the earl think." Maira wanted this nonsense to stop. She wouldn't be swayed by anyone to wed a man against her will.

"Then who will ye marry?" asked Morag.

"No one!" she snapped. "Don't you understand? I'm a warrior, not a feeble noblewoman that will sit at her husband's side like an obedient dog. Besides, no man would want a lady warrior for a wife, just like that man said."

Her eyes roamed over to the gate. Something about the stranger intrigued her yet she couldn't put a finger on why he kept her interest. This man was nothing but a peasant – a mere commoner. He shouldn't have even been talking to her since she was a descendant of the crown. Her thoughts went back to the way his hand felt pressed against hers, and the strong muscles she felt under his tunic when she'd laid her hands on his chest to steady herself. Why did she like it? She'd never felt this way before. And she shouldn't be feeling this way since she was now betrothed to someone else.

An alliance with the High Sheriff of Durham would be a smart move. Her father and the earl were right about that. But this didn't interest her in the least. Instead, all she could think about was the stranger who had held her in his arms so intimately. It was wrong, but Maira now felt like her flirtatious cousin, Willow. Part of her wanted, once again, to be in the stranger's arms even though he was naught but a common thief in the night.

CHAPTER 2

*S*ir Jacob Quincey looked over his shoulder as he rode back to his camp that was located deep in the king's forest. He needed to be more careful. Getting caught stealing, especially by the late king's granddaughter wasn't going to help his cause. Nay, it would only come back to haunt him and bite him in the arse in the end. He couldn't risk such carelessness when his mission was so close to being completed. He wouldn't allow anything or anyone to keep him from his goal. After waiting and preparing for this for three long years, it was finally time to take action.

"Jacob, over here," came a muffled voice from the bushes. Jacob stopped and directed his horse to where his squire, Will, was hiding in wait for him. "Did you get anything we can use?"

"I did." Jacob dismounted, scanned the area and held out the burlap bag to Will. "The iron poker can be used to make a weapon, as well as the gardening tools. I also grabbed a few trinkets as gifts for the women in the village. They are starting to get worried that their husbands and sons will be killed. I thought a gift or two would keep their tongues from wagging and spilling our secret about the upcoming attack. They've all been so good in keeping quiet for so long that I can't have a few last minute scared wenches ruining the only chance I have."

Will took the bag and started to dig through it. "I thought you said you were investigating Castle Rothbury to try to get a hold of some more real weapons. With only our makeshift ones and the ones we've repaired from the battlefield, it's going to be nearly impossible to beat trained soldiers who are well equipped. Did you find a way for us to get in and out of Rothbury without being noticed?"

"I didn't get that far."

"Why not?" Will handed the bag back to Jacob.

"I was distracted."

"By an army? Or was it the earl himself?"

"Neither. It was – it was a girl," he said under his breath, tying the bag to the horse, turning his back to his squire.

"A girl? What girl? Who? And why did you let her distract you?"

"I came across a secret garden and cottage hidden in the woods," he explained. "Something compelled me to go inside. That's where I found these things."

"And you stole them from the girl."

"Nay. I took the things from a dead woman. But while I was there, the girl found me."

"She did? Tell me more."

"I met a beautiful young lady who couldn't have been more than twenty years of age. She was dainty and small with strawberry-blond hair that looked as if it were spun of silk. And her eyes were bright blue like a summer's sky."

"Ah. You probably frightened her."

"I am not so sure. You see, she was as fierce as a lion but, at the same time, I saw innocence within her. She wore a jeweled crown upon her head that looked like it belonged to a queen."

"So, she wasn't a commoner?" Will asked in confusion.

"Nay, not at all. She was a noblewoman."

"Then she had guards and escorts with her."

"Nay again."

"I don't understand. Are you saying she was in the middle of the woods all alone? That doesn't make any sense."

"She certainly was alone. Her name is Lady Maira Douglas. Maira," he repeated, thinking it was the prettiest name he'd ever heard in his life. "She is the daughter of one of the Legendary Bastards of the Crown. I'm not sure which one is her father, but then again it doesn't really matter."

"The Legendary Bastards of the Crown?" gasped Will. "I certainly hope you didn't do anything to anger her. After all, the last thing we need is one of the triplet bastards on our tails when we storm Durham Castle. We're going to have enough trouble just trying to stay alive as it is. Lord Jacob, I'm still not convinced your plan is going to work."

"It has to," said Jacob, climbing atop his horse. "I have no other choice. And I'll remind you again, Will, there's no need to use my title since I no longer hold it." It pained him to say this to his squire, but it was true. He was no longer a lord since the High Sheriff took measures and had Jacob stripped of his title, not to mention his lands. Nay, he was only an outcast now and a petty thief. "I have waited and prepared for this for three long years. I won't wait a minute longer."

"It's a suicide mission and you know it," spat Will. "If we wait a little longer, perhaps we can manage to scrape up enough money to pay a dozen mercenaries to help us."

"There's no time and no way we'll ever attain that kind of money. God's eyes, we've been living off the land like vagrants, lucky to even find food to eat. Unless we stop a noble traveling party, rob them of everything they own and kill them afterwards, it's not going to happen. We're flat broke and you know it."

"Robbing the nobles is a thought." Will looked at him and cocked a half-grin.

Jacob felt a stab go through his heart. He'd already sunk so low that he didn't think he could fall any farther. Chasing after battles through the years like wharf rats living on rancid flesh, he and Will had done the unthinkable by picking through the dead. After the soldiers and camp followers were finished, he and Will snuck in and scavenged whatever they could find. They had only been lucky enough to confiscate weapons that were in disrepair. On occasion, they found a little coin that had been missed.

Jacob hated himself for having to do this, but thanks to the High Sheriff framing him, he had nothing – not even a friend besides Will. He never knew how terrible it felt to be poor or to be an outcast.

It hadn't felt right the first time he slipped a dead man's ring from his finger or pilfered pieces of mail and plate armor. But while building his army, he needed to sell what he could for coin. He used whatever weapons and armor he could and melted down the rest to make what they needed. Still, it wasn't really enough to go up against the wretch that turned Jacob into the pathetic man he was today.

But even so, stealing from nobles on the road was where he stopped. It was too risky. He and Will would be going up against a dozen or two trained soldiers, if not more. They'd either be killed or captured, and he couldn't have either of those happen. He would not allow himself to be beaten and put on display before he was slain. Neither would his corpse be left hanging in the sun for the buzzards to peck at his flesh and eyes. He had mayhap a tiny speck of pride still left in him, and he wasn't going to lose that as well.

"We've got our army waiting in the woods just outside of Durham. With a little luck and some more training with the weapons, I think we can pull this off," Jacob assured him.

"But we're training commoners," Will reminded him.

"True. But look how far they've come in the past three years. I am proud to say with our training, a few of them have mastered the skills better than some soldiers I've known. Besides, we'll have the numbers on our side so I don't believe we'll be captured."

"The numbers?" asked Will. "If we have fifty in our army, I'm exaggerating."

"But you're forgetting something. St. Catherine's Day is approaching. I know for a fact that this feast day is when the wretched High Sheriff, Sir Gregory Arundell, sends most of his men out on the hunt. He has done so the past few years ever since he was made lord of the castle. It is the only time the king allows him to hunt in the royal forest. He keeps only a dozen soldiers on the battlements at this time and sends out not only his hunters, but every knight and able-bodied man he has living within the castle walls."

"Do you think any of the soldiers who serve him now would be loyal to you instead of him if you returned?" asked Will. "After all, you were the late Lord Emery's Captain of the Guard and the men were under your command."

"I am counting on it," Jacob answered. "Before the High Sheriff framed me, the king was going to give me Durham Castle."

"Aye," answered Will. "And you were planning on marrying Lady Catherine even though the late lord of the castle promised his daughter to the High Sheriff."

"Nay. Catherine was never supposed to marry him."

"Really?"

"Sir Gregory talked him into changing his mind. It was all by Arundell's doing that she was taken away from me. There might be loyalty to him from the original knights and soldiers he brought to Durham but there's no love for Arundell from the original men of Durham. Of this, I'm sure. Because of this, and hopefully help from the inside, it will be easy taking back what was supposed to have been mine."

"I hope you're right."

"The man is stupid as well as greedy," Jacob grunted. "My sources tell me that he always stays behind from the hunt. He thinks that he and a dozen soldiers can protect the castle while the others are away. He wants as much game caught as he can get. Every year he invites the Bishop of Durham to his castle for a feast to celebrate. I'm telling you, that is our window of opportunity. The dozen guards on the castle wall walks will be so far in their cups that they won't know what happened. We have to do this. However, once we move forward, there is no turning back."

"We need real soldiers, Jacob. What we have is naught but farmers and peasants," Will complained.

"We have constructed weapons, and repaired weapons from the battlefield. We have what we need to fight. I believe my army is ready."

"But most of them will die going up against trained soldiers. Can you live with that on your conscious?"

"I've told you time and again that it was the choice of every one of the peasants to join me. They hate the High Sheriff almost as much as I do for the way he treats them and taxes them to death."

"I realize the villagers have been mistreated and overtaxed. But Jacob, they are still under the rule of the High Sheriff."

"Don't worry about it, Will."

"This is crazy! I never should have joined you on this mission." Will paced back and forth, worrying like he usually did. "I should have stayed back at Durham Castle and paid fealty to Sir Gregory Arundell. If so, at least I'd have a decent meal and a place inside the great hall by the fire to sleep."

"Getting cold feet, Squire? I've never seen you act this way, not even before battle." Jacob's fury burned in his veins for what he'd been through. But then he realized that he couldn't take out his anger on the boy. Will had been a loyal squire and even stayed with Jacob after he was stripped of not only his title but also his pride. "However, I know it's been hard these past three years. I appreciate the fact you stayed with me, Will. But of course, you know you're free to leave at any time. After all, I'm no one anymore but a thief in the night. I've lost everything because of the High Sheriff. My family has all been killed between war and the plague, except for my worthless brother, and I don't have a penny to my name. Even Lady Catherine is gone now, so there is no chance of me getting her back. I have nothing to offer you at all. Mayhap you should go, as it would be best for you."

Will lowered his head and took a minute to answer. "Nay, I won't leave you." He sighed and kicked at the ground. "We've been together for this long, I won't back out now. I want to help you regain your title as well as claim the castle as your own. After all, you deserve it, not him."

"Thank you, Squire. I knew I could count on you. If I could, I'd make you a knight for your loyalty."

"I would like that," said Will sadly. "Perhaps someday it'll be more than just a wish."

"I hope you're right."

"Sir Jacob, there's got to be an easier way to go about this," said Will. "Are you sure you can't go to the king and explain to him that Arundell framed you?"

"I wish it were that easy but it's his word as well as the Bishop of Durham's against mine." Jacob turned his horse, preparing to leave. "The High Sheriff is a powerful man. If he wants something, he gets it. But I am going to put an end to that soon."

"Then we need more weapons before we return to Durham. The fighting skills of the villagers have improved over the years, but we need more real swords and battleaxes. Not just the makeshift ones we've forged from iron pokers, shovels and old rakes."

"I know." Jacob glanced in the direction of Castle Roth-bury. There was one way to get what he needed and he hoped it would pay off. "We'll go back to camp for the night and tomorrow we'll sneak into Castle Rothbury's armory and take what we need."

Jacob had a good dozen able-bodied men back at camp, not far from where they were. They were hidden in the densest part of the forest. They were only farmers and commoners but that might work to his advantage in this case. No one would be leery of them.

"But how are we going to sneak in?" asked Will. "We don't even know what kind of defenses they have."

"We're not sneaking in," Jacob explained. "We're going to walk right through the front gate."

"We are?" Will shook his head. "I don't understand."

"When we get back to camp, prepare the wagons. Tomorrow, we'll enter the castle's walls under the ploy of being traveling merchants. If we're lucky, we'll leave with a cart full of weapons."

"But how are we going to do that? And why would they let us inside the gates? The earl is sure to know something is amiss."

"I don't think so. I saw one of the king's messengers on the road the other day. I found out that the earl is being called away to campaign for the king. He leaves today. That means the Lady of the Castle will be in charge tomorrow until his return. I have a plan, and the girls are going to help us get inside, whether they know it or not."

"The girls? There was more than one?" asked Will. "I'm confused."

"Aye. There were three others that entered the garden and I believe they were Maira's cousins."

"More daughters of the bastards," grumbled Will with a frustrated sigh. "This isn't a good omen. What makes you think the girls are going to help us get inside the castle walls?"

"Because of this." Will dug through the burlap bag with the things he'd stolen from inside the cottage of the secret garden. He pulled out an item and held it up for Will to see. "I know a lady inside the castle who is going to want this returned. I think we will pay her a little visit."

CHAPTER 3

*M*aira stood in the stable with Morag and Branton, waving to Fia and Willow as they left along with their husbands and their fathers. Willow's wedding celebration had come to an end. Sadly, everyone was going their separate ways. Lord Beaufort and some of his men had left yesterday on their journey to campaign for the king. Even Maira's father, having commitments to attend to, said his goodbyes and headed back to Whitehaven. Already the castle seemed quiet and vacant. But unfortunately, Maira wouldn't have long to enjoy the solitude. At this very moment, her things were being packed and her traveling party was preparing to take her to Durham where she would live for a fortnight with the High Sheriff who was, sadly, her betrothed.

Lady Ernestine, the earl's wife, was in charge until his return. The woman headed into the great hall with her ladies-in-waiting, followed by a group of soldiers that would be protecting her while the earl was gone.

"It seems so empty and lonely here with Fia and Willow both gone now," said Morag.

"It's only going to get worse when we leave in an hour for Durham," Maira told her cousin, feeling sick to her stomach about this whole situation.

"Mayhap it willna be so bad," said Morag, trying to comfort her. "Perhaps like yer faither and the earl said, ye'll get used to the High Sheriff and willna mind marryin' him after all."

"I would rather be strung up from the battlements and have my eyes pecked out by crows than marry the High Sheriff – or any man for that matter." Maira turned and stormed toward the keep to make sure none of her weapons were forgotten. Even if she couldn't use them in front of the High Sheriff, she'd sneak off to the woods with them to practice when he didn't know it.

"Lady Maira." A young pageboy ran up to stop her.

Maira halted abruptly and turned toward the boy. "What is it?"

"The guard at the gate sent me over to fetch you."

"Whatever for?" she asked, anxious to get to her chamber.

"He said one of the travelers has asked for you. They want to sell their wares and they say that they know you and that you will vouch for them."

Maira's eyes shot over to the front gate. There was a traveling party of peasants on foot. Behind them was a cart. A young man drove the wagon. Beside him on the bench was a man covered by a cloak. His hood was up and hid his face from her view.

"Peasants?" asked Maira. "I don't know any peasants. Tell the guard to send them away." She turned to go back to the keep but Morag stopped her with her hand on her arm.

"Are ye no' even a little curious as to why they ask for ye or how they ken ye?"

"Nay, I'm not," snapped Maira.

"I think we should go over there and see who they are." Morag stretched her neck to peruse them, always making everything her business.

"If you'd like to go, then go right ahead but I'm not interested." Maira was about to leave until the man sitting in the cart called out to her and waved his hand.

"Lady Maira, would you like to buy our wares?"

"Nay," she called back. "I'm not interested."

"I think I have something you want. It's a heart with your name on it."

"Maira, ye've got to go look." Morag urged her to join the strangers as she tugged on Maira's sleeve. "It sounds intriguin'."

"Let go of me, Morag." Maira shook out of her hold. "I am sure the stranger is just making it up. He doesn't have a heart with my name on it. Why would he?"

"Lady Maira, look at this." Branton walked over, inspecting something clutched in his fingers. "That traveler asked me to show it to you."

"Branton, I am not interested in anything that –" Maira stopped in midsentence when she saw the item in Branton's hand. It was a small wooden heart with holes on each side. In the center of the heart was Maira's name carved right into it. "Let me see that." Maira snatched it out of Branton's hold to inspect it.

"He sent this one over, too. It has Willow's name on it." Branton held up a second wooden heart.

"It does?" asked Morag excitedly. "What about me? Does he have a heart with my name on it, too?"

"Nay, he said these were the only two," said Branton, inspecting the heart with Willow's name on it.

"I've seen this before," said Maira, feeling anxious.

"That looks like the heart that was on the bracelet we made for Fia," Morag told her.

"Aye, it certainly does." Maira knew exactly where this came from. Her attention flashed back to the man sitting in the cart. He noticed and reached up to lower his hood so she could see his face. Maira's jaw dropped open.

"Maira, are these the hearts that Imanie made?" asked Morag, inspecting Willow's heart. "Ye ken what I mean. Are they the ones ye said she was makin' into bracelets that ye'd each get someday?"

"How could they be?" asked Branton. "Why would that peasant have them?"

"Branton, go to our chamber and get our bags. Please load them on the cart," Maira instructed. Her eyes stayed fastened to the man on the wagon who was none other than the thief she met in the secret garden.

"Did I tell you that the earl is sending me to Durham with you two?" asked Branton.

"That's nice," said Maira, not even listening to him.

"Let's go talk to the stranger," said Morag. "I want to find out if he has a heart for me, too."

"I'm sure he doesn't, and you're not coming with me. Now go," Maira commanded, not wanting Morag to know the thief was inside the castle walls. If so, she would tell Lady Ernestine. Maira didn't want that. She needed to know what he wanted first.

"I'm always forgotten," pouted Morag, leaving with Branton and heading into the keep.

Maira hurried over to the wagon, nodding to the guard to let the traveling party enter. Once they were inside, the peasants started pulling things off the cart to sell. It was odd since they only had a couple of buckets of berries and a few odd trinkets.

"Lady Maira, we meet again." The man swung down from the wagon and landed right in front of her. Her eyes interlocked with his. Instantly, she felt the same attraction she'd experienced when he'd almost kissed her in the garden.

"What is the meaning of this?" she sniffed.

"We're peddlers and here to sell our wares. Thank you for vouching for us."

One of the men took a few things off the hay-covered wagon. He dropped something and it went clattering to the ground. Maira looked over to see him picking up the poker that had been stolen from Imanie's cottage.

"These things are not yours to sell, and you know it," she said in a low voice. "Now leave Imanie's items, and get out of here at once."

"My, you are feisty in everything you say and do." The man took her by the elbow. "Shall we go for a little walk?"

"Nay, we shall not." She pulled out of his grip. When she did, she dropped the wooden heart. He bent over and picked it up, caressing her name on the heart with his thumb. For some reason, a shiver ran through her. It was such an intimate action and she felt as if he were doing it to her physically.

"If you don't want to buy this, then I think I will give it to you as a token of my appreciation for letting us inside the castle walls."

"I'm sure it was a mistake," she retorted. "I already regret it. Now pack up your cart and leave at once."

"That, my lady, is exactly what I intend to do. However, my friends are hungry. Since we haven't had any real food in days, I ask that you allow us to stay for a meal before we retreat."

"Why would I do that?"

"Because it's the right thing to do." He reached up and yanked at a leather tie holding back his long hair. His dark mane spilled down, loose, around his shoulders. He was very handsome and she tried to push the thought from her mind because she wanted him to leave.

He took the wooden heart with her name on it and pushed the leather thong through the holes and held it up. "Hold out your wrist," he instructed.

Without knowing why she did it, she raised her hand and he tied the bracelet around her wrist. It felt good to be getting a present from a man, even though it was with an item that he'd pilfered.

"It is becoming, but could never match the beauty of you, my lady."

"Thank you," she said, reaching down and running her hand over the bracelet that was made with the tie from his hair. Her hand brushed against his and a jolt of excitement rushed through her. Then she quickly pulled away and stepped back.

"Lady Maira?" asked Lady Ernestine, coming across the courtyard to meet her. "Lady Morag tells me there is a traveler here with a wooden heart with your name on it. What does she mean?"

"Aye," said Maira, clearing her throat and trying to figure

out what to do. But before she could say another word, the thief stepped forward and bowed.

"My good Lady of the Castle, I thank you for letting us enter into your courtyard to sell our wares," he said. "I brought the good Lady Maira a present of thanks for the last time she threw us a coin while her entourage was passing through the forest."

"I see." Lady Ernestine looked to Maira for confirmation.

"Aye," said Maira, not wanting her to know she allowed thieves into her courtyard. "It was a nice gesture, but unfortunately they have to leave."

"Leave?" asked Lady Ernestine. "But they haven't even sold any of their wares yet."

"That's right," said the man. "And how soon you forget, Lady Maira, that you invited my friends and me to stay for a meal."

Her eyes snapped up and she was about to object when Lady Ernestine spoke.

"I think that is a wonderful idea. I love feeding those less fortunate than myself," said the good-hearted woman. "What is your name?"

"I am Jacob, my lady. And might I be bold enough to offer you a token of my appreciation?" He dug through his pocket.

"Oh, that's not necessary." Lady Ernestine swiped her hand through the air and a blush rose to her cheeks.

"It isn't much, but can I offer you a small bauble?" He held out a lady's comb to wear in her hair. It had a small gold butterfly on the handle.

"Oh, that is charming and I do love butterflies," she exclaimed. Jacob held up his open palm and the woman took the gift from him. "Lady Maira, please see that our guests get whatever they need during their short stay."

"But Lady Ernestine, I am leaving in an hour unless you forgot. I still need to finishing packing my belongings."

"Your trip can wait until after the meal and until our guests leave."

"I would love Lady Maira to give me a tour of your elegant castle if it is convenient," said Jacob with a charming smile.

"It isn't," Maira mumbled to herself.

"'Tis no trouble at all," Lady Ernestine beamed. "Lady Maira will escort you around the grounds. Now, if you'll excuse me, I'll tell the cook we'll be expecting a few more guests for the meal." She turned and left, pushing the comb into her hair as she walked.

JACOB TURNED and grinned at Maira, but she was scowling at him.

"How dare you give away stolen goods to buy your way into the castle," she said in a hoarse whisper. "I should turn you in right now and expose who you really are."

"You have no idea who I am," he scoffed. He held out his arm like she'd expect from a nobleman and she instinctively laid her hand over it to be escorted, not knowing why she did it. "Besides," he continued, "the goods belong to a dead woman so I hardly call that stealing."

"Imanie might be dead but I can vouch that these are her things," she retorted as they headed to the keep.

"I'd like to see the armory first," he told her, ignoring her comment altogether. "After that, the blacksmith's shop, and the stables."

"Why should I show you anything? You have no right to come in here and make demands."

"I see." He nodded slowly and studied the castle. "So, you didn't like my gift to you?"

"I like the bracelet, but that is beside the point."

"Then, what is the point, my lady?"

"The point is that . . . that . . . you have me so confused. I'm not sure what the point is anymore."

"Then let's stick to the tour because I won't be staying long and don't want to miss the meal."

MAIRA RELUCTANTLY GAVE the stranger named Jacob a tour of Castle Rothbury, only because Lady Ernestine had instructed her to do so. She had a bad feeling about this man and needed to keep a close eye on him. She didn't trust him any further than she could throw him. They walked in silence as they entered the first building attached to the battlements.

"This is the armory," she said, watching his eyes light up as he surveyed the weapons inside. He walked over and picked up a sword and looked down the edge, squinting one eye.

"I haven't seen weapons this nice in a long time." He tested the weight of the blade in his hand.

"When have you ever seen weapons like these at all?" she asked, suspiciously.

"A long time ago," he said, picking up a battle axe and surveying it next. "Where is all the chain mail and plate armor?"

"Most of that has been taken by Lord Beaufort."

"Ah, yes. I guess fighting overseas for the king calls for

greater protection. I also suppose that's why most of the weapons are gone."

"How did you know the earl went to fight overseas for the king?"

"You told me," he said. "In the garden," he added, sounding a little nervous if she wasn't mistaken.

Maira was sure she hadn't told him that the earl was leaving, so that meant he had to have been spying on her or gotten the information in another way. He wasn't inside the castle walls long enough for anyone to have divulged that fact to him.

"Oh, that's right. I did tell you," she lied, watching for his reaction. If Fia were there, she would have been able to read the man's mind and know his secrets just by the way he responded. She ran a finger along the table, keeping her eyes downcast. "It was right before you tried to kiss me."

"What?" He lowered the sword and his eyes shot over to her.

"You tried to kiss me, but I wouldn't let you. Don't you remember? Thank goodness you didn't persist or I would have had to take you down."

"Take me down," he said under his breath with a chuckle. "The day I'm taken down by a wench the size of you is the day I turn into a pitiful, pathetic shell of a man. You could never do it, so don't even pretend that you could." He picked up a dagger next and inspected it.

She wanted more than anything to prove him wrong, and the competitive side of her made her bold enough to take the challenge. She sidled up next to him, putting her hands on his arm. He turned to look at her. This was her chance. She tried to act like her cousin Willow who always used to flirt with the men before she married Conrad. Maira batted her eyelashes and tried to talk in a soft, feminine, sing-song voice.

"I wish you had kissed me," she said, noticing he was taking the bait.

"Really?" He put down the weapon and did a quick scan of the room and door to make sure no one was coming.

"Really," she said, pressing up close to him and lifting her eyes, keeping her head down, trying to act shy. "Don't you wonder what it would be like to kiss me?"

"I think I'm about to find out." Jacob reached out and put his hand under her chin, lifting her mouth to his. She hadn't actually meant to kiss him, but something about him was so alluring that she had to know how his lips tasted. The kiss was soft and warm. It isn't at all what she expected from a thief. Plus it was gentle for a man who was used to taking whatever he wanted without asking.

"Mmmm," he mumbled, coming back for a second helping. Suddenly, Maira realized how foolish she was being. She couldn't let him kiss her again. Taking a hold of his arm in a tight grip, she turned to the side and used her shoulder and hip to set him off balance. She managed to flip him around and push him to the ground. He landed with an outtake of air from his mouth when his back hit the rushes. In one motion, Maira drew her dagger, wishing for her sword that was being shined by Branton in the stable. She put one foot on his chest and leaned forward, holding the tip of her dagger to his neck.

"Today is the day," she snarled. "Know that you have been taken by a woman half your size. So, I guess this makes you naught but a pitiful, pathetic shell of a man after all, doesn't it?"

"Nice move," he said, raising his brows. "I must say you

41

never cease to surprise me. I've never met a wench quite like you before."

"I'm not a wench, I'm a lady!" she retorted. "And you have severely underestimated me. You'd be best to remember that in the future. Now, whatever game you are playing, I warn you, it's not going to work. Gather up your men and leave now while you still can."

"Lady Maira, you are a clever woman and very skilled at fighting. However, I must tell you that you have underestimated me as well."

In one move, he had Maira down on the floor on her back and was kneeling over her. He pressed the edge of a jewel-hilted dagger to her throat. She had never seen this weapon before. He hadn't pilfered it in the armory. Nay, he pulled it out from under his cloak and had it all along.

"Get off of me and let me up," she cried. "Do it, or I will call for the guards to haul you away to the dungeon for assaulting me."

"Now, now, it doesn't have to come to that." He stuck his weapon into his waist belt and with one strong arm, pulled her to her feet. He did it with such momentum that she barreled into his chest. His arms closed around her and before she knew what was happening, his lips were on hers again.

"Stop it," she said, pushing out of his arms and slapping him hard across the cheek. "I don't know who you think you are, but I've never been treated like this before by a peasant!"

"Nay? Then how about by a nobleman or a knight?" he asked, making her wonder what he meant by that.

"Where did you get that dagger?" Her eyes settled at his waist as she surveyed the jeweled piece. It was exquisite and she longed to see it closer.

"You like it?" he asked, removing it again and holding it out for her to see. "Go ahead and feel the weight of it in your palm. It's made from Damascus steel. The gems were from my – from the necklace of a noblewoman."

"Oh, so you stole this, too." She took the dagger in her hand and marveled at how light it was. "My sword is made from Damascus steel as well," she told him. "My father paid a lot of money to have it constructed by a bladesmith overseas. However, I don't have any daggers made from that material. It's so balanced and light yet it looks so sharp. It is the most beautiful weapon I have ever seen."

"It can gut a man in less than ten seconds and still be sharp enough to scalp the next man with little effort at all."

Maira felt sick with the visual of that in her head. She was good at sparring and using weapons but had never killed anything other than a rabbit or pheasant, the largest thing being a deer. Thinking how excited this man sounded at ripping into another man's flesh made her leery of being alone with him.

"I think it's time for the meal," she said, hearing a small squeak in her voice. "Here, take back your dagger and let's go."

He retrieved the dagger, letting his fingers purposely touch hers in the exchange. It sent a tingle flitting across her skin. Her lips still vibrated from his kiss and the blood pumped furiously through her body from the rush of excitement coursing through her from their sparring. Her eyes stayed fastened to the dagger as he attached it to his belt and hid it again with his cloak. She loved Damascus steel but it was rare and very expensive. With the gems in the hilt of that dagger, it looked like he'd stolen it from a noble, or perhaps even the king.

He cleared his throat, causing her gaze to meet his. Steel gray eyes warmed her to her very soul.

"I see the way you look at my weapon. You must like it very much."

"It's amazing. I've never seen one like it before."

He chuckled. "That's what most women tell me in the midst of heated passion."

She suddenly realized he was making a jest of the whole situation. Or perhaps he had really been talking about his manhood instead of his dagger all along.

"You're not funny," she ground out. "Now get moving, and I warn you, don't even think of touching me again."

JACOB QUICKLY SURVEYED the layout of the area, noticing after they saw the blacksmith's shop and the stable that most of the guards on the wall were gone. A bell rang out for the second time, and everyone disappeared into the great hall. "What was that?" he asked.

"It's time for the meal," she explained. "You'd better gather your friends and come to the great hall because the food goes fast."

"Is that where all the guards on the wall walk went?" he asked casually.

"Aye, Lady Ernestine is adamant about feeding everyone. The guard left at the watchtower will eat when the rest are finished."

"I see," he said with a satisfied nod. "Go on inside and I'll meet you there. I will just help my friends pack up the wares and we'll be there in a few minutes."

"All right. I'll let Lady Ernestine know." She headed away

into the great hall and Jacob watched her go. Then he turned and walked as fast as he could without running and causing suspicion.

"Will," he said when he approached the wagon. "Round up the others and get to the armory right away. Bring the wagon to the front gate. We have a few minutes only to load the weapons into the cart and hightail it out of here before the guards return."

"Are you sure we won't be stopped?" asked Will nervously.

"There's only one guard at the watchtower. I'll take him out first and then we'll load up what we need and be out of here before anyone even eats their main course."

"Oh, so we're not staying for the meal?" asked Will, sounding extremely disappointed. His stomach growled loudly, protesting as well.

"Nay, we're not here for food or did you forget our purpose?"

"All right. I'll bring the wagon around and tell the men."

"Good." Jacob scanned the battlements quickly just to make sure there were no more guards. "Be quiet about it," he whispered. "We don't want to alert anyone. I'll get up to the watch tower and take care of the guard."

"Sounds good." Will hurried off to do his job while Jacob turned and headed to the stairs of the battlements.

"Oh, there ye are," came a female voice from behind him, stopping him in his tracks.

He turned around to see Maira's cousin, Morag, and flinched. She was going to ruin everything. "Aye. Hello."

"Are ye comin' for the meal?" she asked. "After all, ye were invited. We're havin' haggis today at my request. Lady Ernestine kens I miss my homeland of Scotland so she has the cook make food from my homeland as often as possible." Morag droned on and on, taking up much of Jacob's precious time.

"Aye, that's nice," he said, trying to get rid of her quickly. He saw Will moving the wagon into position. The rest of his men headed up to the armory, sneaking up the stairs in the shadows. "I . . . need to use the garderobe and I'll be right there." He turned the girl by her shoulders so she wouldn't notice what was going on. "You go on back to the great hall."

"But the garderobe is this way," said Morag, pointing in the opposite direction.

"I can't wait. I'm actually going to use the orchard. So you'd better leave unless you want to see my bare –"

"I'm goin'," she said, holding a hand up to the side of her face to block her view and hurrying into the great hall to join the rest. Thank goodness, he managed to get rid of her, but she had slowed him down.

He ran up the stairs and over to the watchtower, throwing open the door. To his surprise, he found not only the guard but also Maira inside.

"I thought you'd end up here," said Maira, leaning back on a chair with her arms crossed over her chest. "Guard, he's a thief and here to steal from us. Put him in the dungeon." She stood and pointed an accusing finger at Jacob.

The guard moved forward, but Jacob held up his hands. "Now wait a minute, my lady. I saw you come up here so I came to escort you to the great hall. That is all."

"He doesn't seem to have a weapon on him, my lady," said the guard, trying to peruse him. "Perhaps he tells the truth."

"He's got a dagger hidden under his cloak," she informed the man.

"Nay, I don't," Jacob answered, hands still in the air. "Go ahead and check if you'd like."

The guard stepped forward to search him. Jacob took advantage of the situation by knocking the man out with a punch to the face. Maira watched with wide eyes. If the guard had tried to attack him, Jacob might have had to use his blade and it could have been deadly. But seeing Maira's face, he realized he couldn't kill a man in front of her. It just wouldn't seem right. Instead, he punched the man again, just to make sure he stayed down.

Maira's eyes met with his and, for a moment, the world stood still. Neither of them moved. Her gaze lowered to his mouth telling him she was thinking about the kiss they had shared. He was thinking about it, too. But then the moment was broken when she went for her sword fastened to her back that hadn't been there during their tour of the castle. Jacob snapped out of the momentary trance he'd been in and managed to move faster than her. With one kick, he knocked the sword from her hand and it slid across the floor with a loud clang. Then he grabbed her wrists and some rope from the wall and tied her hands together.

"You should have gone to the great hall, my lady, instead of retrieving your sword and coming here. It pains me to do this, but I can't let you ruin my mission."

Will stuck his head in the door just then. "The weapons are loaded and we're ready to go," he said, looking first at the guard on the floor and then at Maira. "What's going on here?"

"Lady Maira is going to be tied up for a while or I'd ask her to join us," Jacob answered

"Guards!" Maira shouted, but Jacob clamped his hand over

her mouth. "Will, give me something to use as a gag. I won't have her calling out again and alerting everyone we're here."

"Use this," said Will, tossing a tunic to him from a hook on the wall. Jacob pushed Maira down in a chair and then ripped the tunic, shoving it into her mouth.

"Nay, don't –"

He cut her off short, reaching around her to tie her to the chair.

"Go to the wagon quickly," Jacob told Will over his shoulder. "Get over the drawbridge fast because someone might have heard her and think to close the gate."

"What about you, my lord?" asked Will.

Jacob noticed Maira look up, hearing Will use his title. He clenched his jaw and shook his head, wanting to wring the boy's neck for calling him that in front of her. "Leave the extra horse. I'll follow in a minute. Now go!"

"Aye," said Will, running out the door.

Jacob felt Maira press up closer to him as he tied her tighter. The blasted feel of her hands against him made him randy. All he could think about was kissing her again, but this should be the last thing on his mind at a time like this.

"Until we meet again, my lady," said Jacob, fondly running his fingers over her cheek, and then turning and heading out the door.

MAIRA PULLED the man's jewel-hilted dagger out from the folds of her gown, holding the blade between her tied hands. The fool didn't even know she took it. For being a thief, he was not very good at his profession or he would have felt an amateur pilfering his weapon. She used it first to cut the gag from around her mouth. "Sebastian, get up," she called out to the guard. "Wake up! I need your help."

The guard stirred and moaned as Maira tried to cut the ropes on her hands but at the angle of the blade, it was impossible. Since the thief didn't tie her feet, she was able to stand. With the chair still tied to her, she walked over and kicked the guard.

"Get up! We've been robbed," she shouted.

Sebastian's eyes fluttered open and he jumped to his feet.

"Lady Maira, did he hurt you?" He pulled his dagger from his belt and cut her free from her bindings.

"Nay, and you are lucky he didn't kill you."

"Aye. I wonder why he didn't."

"We can speculate about that later. Right now, we need to tell Lady Ernestine that we've been robbed. She'll have to send out a search party right away."

"She won't do that," said Sebastian with a shake of his head.

"But she has to. They stole weapons, I'm sure of it."

"Lady Maira, you don't understand. There aren't enough soldiers left at Castle Rothbury right now to pursue this. If the earl and the rest of the men were here, it would be a different story. But with the little forces we have on hand right now, we need to stay and protect Lady Ernestine and defend the castle."

"Lady Maira, are you all right?" asked Lady Ernestine, hurrying into the guard house with Morag and Branton right behind her.

"Lady Ernestine." Maira rushed over to meet her. "That man, Jacob, who gave you the present was naught but a thief. He and his men robbed us."

"I know," she answered. "Morag told me she saw Jacob going up the guardhouse and that she thought something was wrong."

"We've got to go after him," said Maira, anxious to hunt them down.

"I can't give that order," said Lady Ernestine. "My garrison of soldiers is sparse since my husband took most of them to fight for the king. And I'll need to send some of them to guard you and Morag on the way to Durham."

"So, you're just going to let the man get away with stealing from us?"

"He couldn't have taken much," said Lady Ernestine. "When my husband returns, he'll address the issue. But at this time, there is nothing I can do about it."

"That's just not right," said Maira, fingering the thief's jewel-handled dagger, inspecting it as she spoke.

"What's that?" asked Morag, being as curious as always.

"It's the thief's dagger," Maira told her.

"Did he drop it?" asked Branton.

"Nay," Maira said with a smile. "I lifted it from him when he was tying me up."

"So ye stole it from him, just like he stole from us," said Morag.

"Let's just say this is payback for what he took from us."

"You mean for the weapons he stole," said Branton.

"Well, that, too," she said, really talking about the kiss he stole from her that she had never meant to give him.

CHAPTER 4

"We did it," said Will excitedly once they got back to camp. "We managed to get real weapons. These will come in handy for the attack."

The half-dozen men with them all inspected the swords, daggers, and battle axes they'd stolen from Castle Rothbury.

"We should have a fighting chance now," said one of the villagers named Roger.

"I can't wait to try this beauty." Gerald, another of the villagers who Jacob had trained to fight, swiped the sword through the air.

"Let me swing a battle axe," said another of the men eagerly.

"Nay," said Jacob, dismounting his horse. "There'll be time for that later. Right now we need to get back and distribute these weapons amongst our army. The time is approaching fast, and we'll have only one chance to attack the High Sheriff and claim the castle."

"Then let's go," said Gerald, tossing the sword into the back of the wagon.

Out of habit, Jacob's hand reached for his lucky dagger that once belonged to his mother. He, in return had given it to his lover, Lady Catherine. It was the only thing he had left that the High Sheriff hadn't taken from him. When his hand came up empty, he pushed away his cloak, patting his weapon belt, but the dagger was not there.

"Damnation, I do not believe this," he cursed.

"What is the matter?" Will climbed up to the bench seat of the wagon.

"My dagger. It's missing."

"Mayhap you dropped it when you tied up the girl," suggested Will.

"The girl," Jacob repeated, his jaw clenching tightly. He remembered her reaching out to touch him in what he foolishly thought was a seductive move. Now he knew exactly why she did it. She was stealing his prized possession. He hadn't even realized it.

"God's eyes, she tricked me!" He kicked at a rock and it went flying. Roger ducked to keep from being hit.

"What's got you so upset, Jacob?" asked Gerald.

"I have been made a fool of and I don't fancy that," he spat. "Will, take the wagon back and have the villagers practice with the new weapons."

"Aye, my lord," said Will, calling him by his title out of habit. "But where will you be?"

"I've got a little side errand to run that shouldn't take too long. I'll meet back with you later tonight. But right now, I need to pay a little visit to someone who is not going to be happy to see me."

* * *

AN HOUR LATER, Maira was on her way to Durham Castle. Morag, Branton, three guards, and a servant driving the cart with their trunks accompanied her. They headed out the castle gates on their way to meet with her betrothed.

Maira's sword was strapped to her back even though her father had told her to hide her weapons from Sir Gregory Arundell. She no longer cared. She also carried two daggers attached to her waist belt, plus the one she'd pilfered from the thief. It irked her that she had been tied up by the man when she had every chance to capture him and have him thrown into the dungeon. But she had hesitated and, in that moment, he was able to get the better of her. Hadn't her father always told her not to hesitate when making a decision? If so, it could cost someone's life.

"Maira, wait up," called out Morag, riding to her side. Maira rode the horse astride, but Morag rode in a sidesaddle the way that was expected of a lady. They both wore gowns made of taffeta and silk lined with lace. Lady Ernestine had insisted they look their best when they met the High Sheriff. Maira didn't care about looking good, but she did it out of respect to the woman who was her guardian. "What happened with the thief?" she asked.

"What do you mean?" Maira scanned their surroundings as they headed down a path that led right through the woods. It was a likely place for thieves and bandits to be lying in wait and she wouldn't be taken by surprise again.

"The man named Jacob," said Morag, pulling Maira from her thoughts. "What did he do to ye?"

Maira's heart skipped a beat at hearing this question. All she could think about was Jacob's kiss. She needed to tell someone about it or she was going to burst. Morag wasn't her first choice of who to confide in, but since Fia and Willow were married now and no longer available to talk with, Maira had no other choice. It was Morag or no one at all. She couldn't keep this secret to herself any longer, so decided to talk to her cousin.

"He kissed me," Maira blurted out, hoping she hadn't made a mistake by telling the biggest gossip in the castle her intimate secret.

"He did what?" asked Morag with wide eyes.

"You heard me. Jacob kissed me. And I have to say . . . I liked it."

"Who kissed you?" asked Branton, overhearing her and riding up next to her at her other side.

"Maira kissed the thief," said Morag, already running her mouth.

"Morag, quiet," spat Maira. "That was supposed to be a secret between us."

"Oh. I dinna ken it was a secret." Morag shrugged her shoulders. "Ye should have mentioned that."

Maira had no patience for her silly cousin today. "You don't deserve to wear that heart brooch because you will never be a true member of the Followers of the Secret Heart, even if you think you are. You need to be able to keep a secret, and we all know you couldn't do that if your life depended on it."

"That's no' true," cried Morag.

"You're talking about that secret group that the queen chose you for, aren't you?" asked Branton.

"Maira, you shouldna be talkin' about the secret group." Morag scolded Maira now. "Ye are no better than me."

"I only mentioned it because Branton already knows about

it," Maira pointed out. "Besides, it probably no longer matters." Her hand went to the heart brooch pinned on her chest. "With Fia and Willow gone, I'm the last member now. There isn't much I can do by myself."

"Ye've got me," whined Morag. "Ye are no' alone, Maira. Mayhap, together we can hunt down that thief and get the weapons back. That would be a guid thing to do, wouldna it?"

"Hah!" spat Branton. "Not unless you two want to lose your lives. Otherwise, it is the stupidest idea I've ever heard. You couldn't possibly accomplish that on your own. Besides, it's much too dangerous."

"Then ye will help us," Morag told Branton.

"Me?" His hand went to his chest. "I was sent by the earl to keep an eye on you two and that is just what I intend to do. I highly doubt if I turned to hunting down thieves that the earl will ever make me a squire."

"You will never be a squire anyway," said Maira with a sigh. "If the earl had intended to do that, it would be done by now."

"Not so," said Branton, raising his chin. "I have what it takes to be a squire and it's any time now that the earl will recognize my skills and do something about it."

Maira shook her head. "We'll have to forget about the thief because that is no longer an option. Besides, I have more important things to do than to waste my time with this."

"More important? Like what?" asked Morag.

"Aye. I'd like to know the answer to that, too," chimed in Branton.

"I'll tell you what," said Maira with a determined nod of her head. "I need to find a way to break my betrothal with the High Sheriff."

"But Maira, ye dinna have to marry him," Morag reminded her. "Ye ken that our grandda, King Edward III, gave ye permission to marry a man of yer choosin'."

"Aye," said Maira, touching the jeweled crown on her head that was given to her as a child. It used to be Queen Philippa's crown. Maira's cousins, Fia and Willow, each received a crown as well when they were young children. "I understand that, but I also know that the earl has great influence over my father and he happens to think my marrying the High Sheriff would be a good alliance. I also have a feeling the High Sheriff is a very powerful and influential man. It isn't going to be easy to get out of this betrothal."

"Then marry the man," said Branton nonchalantly. "You are past marrying age and he is titled, powerful, and rich. What are you waiting for?"

"I am twenty years of age and he is close to forty, or so I've been told." Maira didn't like this idea at all. "He's not the type of man I would ever want to marry."

"But you have never even met him," stated Branton. "How can you say that?"

"I just know," she said, thinking about Jacob and his kiss. Why did the man attract her so much? Something inside her felt so alive every time he was near.

"She wants to marry that thief," said Morag, causing Maira to turn so fast in the saddle that she almost lost her balance.

"Nay, I don't want to marry a thief, Morag. Now, I warn you both to keep your mouths closed about what I told you. I don't want to hear Jacob's name mentioned again. Do you understand?"

Without waiting for them to answer, she kicked her heels into the sides of her horse and rode quickly to the front of the line. It was impossible now to think of anything else but the man who robbed them . . . and stole a kiss from her as well.

* * *

"A RE you sure that Lady Maira isn't within the castle walls?" Jacob talked to the young lad outside the gates of Castle Rothbury. He made sure to stay hidden in the shadows so no one would recognize him as the thief. When he saw a young page coming down the path he stopped him to find out what he needed to know.

"I'm sure," said the boy. "I'm a page at the castle. I helped carry Lady Maira and Lady Morag's trunks to the wagon an hour ago."

"They were going somewhere?"

"Aye. Lady Maira is goin' to meet with her betrothed."

"Betrothed," he mumbled, the word upsetting him for some reason. "Do you happen to know who she is marrying? And where she is going?"

"I don't know the man's name but I heard him mentioned as the High Sheriff."

"What?" Jacob stood upright. "What High Sheriff? Of where?" It couldn't be. There had to be a lot of High Sheriffs in England and he was sure it was just a coincidence.

"I knew where it was but I forgot. I think it was somewhere like . . . Dunam or Dover, I can't remember. It was somewhere that started with a D." The page scratched his head in thought and looked up toward the sky.

"Was it . . . Durham Castle by any chance?"

The boy slapped his hands together. "By the rood, that's it. Durham Castle. I remember it now."

"God's eyes, anywhere but there." Jacob dragged a frustrated hand through his hair. Didn't he have enough trouble without having to hear this today?

"Why do you ask?" The boy looked at him suspiciously. "You look familiar. Have you been inside the walls of Castle Rothbury lately?"

"I'm not who you think I am." Jacob pulled a penny from his pouch and handed it to the boy. "And I'd appreciate you keeping your mouth shut about seeing me."

The boy looked up and his eyes opened wide. "I do remember you now. You're that thief that stole our weapons."

"Here's a shilling, now keep your mouth shut." Jacob slapped the coin into the boy's hand and watched his excited expression.

"Aye, I won't say a word," answered the boy, turning and running down the road.

Jacob made his way back to his horse, feeling a knot forming in his stomach. Why did the girl have to be betrothed to Sir Gregory Arundell? Wasn't it enough that the man had already stolen from him anything that had ever mattered in his life? If Jacob didn't like Maira so much, perhaps he wouldn't care. But after kissing her and seeing the way she could handle a blade, it made him want her even more. He couldn't envision anyone else having her but him.

He mounted his horse and rode like hell, trying to catch up to Maira's traveling party. But the page said she left over an hour ago. It was at least a four-hour ride to Durham. If he wanted to catch her before she got to the castle, luck was going to have to be on his side.

CHAPTER 5

"Let's pick up the pace," Maira called out to the others, seeing the threatening black clouds overhead as soon as they exited the forest. "It's going to storm and I don't fancy arriving at Castle Durham dripping wet."

Morag rode to her side. "Maira, I thought ye didna care how ye looked when ye met the High Sheriff."

"I don't," answered Maira, glancing over her shoulder. "I didn't want to say anything, but I get the feeling we are being followed. I am glad we made it through the woods without being attacked by bandits. However, I will feel safer once we are inside the safety of the castle walls."

"I never thought I'd see ye run from danger, Maira."

"I'm not running from danger," she snapped. "After all, I'm riding right into the lion's den, or did you forget? If I can't figure out a way to make the High Sheriff change his mind about marrying me, even with my right to choose my husband, I think this is going to be a nasty situation that I would rather avoid."

"I felt a drop of rain." Morag raised her hood over her

head, not liking to be cold or wet. Maira, on the other hand, liked the outdoors and welcomed nature and any kind of weather.

"I see the castle up ahead," Maira told her. "If we pick up the pace we can make it inside before the storm."

"I bet I could beat ye there," said Morag, being her mischievous self.

"Nay, you could never outride me," answered Maira. "Not while riding sidesaddle."

"I'll race ye," said Morag, taking off before she even waited for Maira's reply. Maira glanced over her shoulder once more, swearing she heard thundering hoofbeats in the distance. Then, as Branton rode by, she urged her horse into a full run.

"Out of the way, Branton. I've got a challenge to win and no one is going to stop me once I make up my mind to accomplish something."

* * *

"Jacob, wait for us," called out Will, driving the cart with the weapons much too fast over the rocky road through the forest.

Jacob kept getting glimpses of Maira and her traveling party, but every time he had to slow down and wait for Will and his men, he lost her again. He finally managed to get close enough behind them to see Maira, Morag, Branton, and the rest of the party just up ahead. If he moved quickly, he could hopefully manage to catch up with them and somehow get Lady Maira separated from the group. Then he would be able to get his dagger returned.

Lightning flashed across the sky followed by a loud crash of thunder that scared the horse pulling the wagon.

"Whoa, girl, whoa," shouted Will, trying to hold back the horse as it reared up on two legs. "Jacob, help!" called out the squire, losing control.

Jacob brought his horse to an abrupt stop as the sky opened up and the rain pelted down all around them. He looked back to see that the wagon lost a wheel and the horse was pulling Will and the damaged cart through the forest aimlessly. Will was unable to stop the skittish horse.

"Dammit, not now." Jacob glanced back the other way to see Maira and the others pick up their pace. They rode at full speed toward the castle. There was nothing he could do about it now. He turned and headed his horse back toward Will. Reaching out, he grabbed the reins, stopping the skittish mare. The rest of his men rode up from behind to help.

"We're nearing camp," said Roger. "After the rain lets up, we can get the others to come back with tools and spokes to help change the broken wheel."

"Nay, we'll do it now," said Jacob. "We can't risk that someone will see our wagon on the road and find our camp. Men, take the weapons back to camp on horseback and fetch some tools and supplies. The wagon is in a ditch and it will take several of us to pull it out. Will and I will calm the horse and find whatever pieces we left in our path. I don't want a trail leading right to our hidden camp."

"What about the girl?" asked Will, nodding toward Durham Castle in the distance. "Are you just going to let her keep your dagger?"

"For now," he said, peering down the road, knowing he would have to enter the castle to retrieve his blade now. "I am going to collect everything that belongs to me as well as everything I want."

"Want?" Will raised an eyebrow. "Please don't tell me you want Lady Maira, my lord. That would make for a very uncomfortable situation."

"Then prepare to be uncomfortable, Squire." Jacob clenched his jaw glancing in the direction of Durham Castle. "I have decided I want Lady Maira, and I won't let the High Sheriff marry her. Nay, I will have her if it's the last thing I ever do."

* * *

RIDING into the courtyard of Durham Castle, Maira felt like she was riding to her doom. Rain fell fast and heavy, making her shiver as she entered through the front gates. The wall walks were lined with guards. Servants bustled about, hurrying to get out of the torrential downpour. A stableboy led several horses to the barn while the kennelgroom rounded up the hounds. The storm came upon them fast and caught everyone unprepared.

Durham Castle sat high upon a hill overlooking a valley that led into the forest. Even in the rain it was a majestic sight to see. The huge stone structure seemed to have a chapel connected as she could see the ornate windows that even had colored glass. That was a very expensive addition that usually was reserved for men with much wealth, the clergy, or the king himself.

The many turrets and the fortress of thick walls surrounded her, making her feel trapped from the moment she rode under the large iron gate. The High Sheriff must be a very wealthy man, indeed. Inside the courtyard were many out buildings and off to the side was a very large stable to house the horses. She was interested to see more but, right now, all she wanted to do was to get in out of the rain. It had been a long and tiresome journey and she was hungry and cold.

"Might I take your horse, my lady?" A young boy dressed in a thin wet tunic with bare feet ran up and held out his hands for the reins. She figured he couldn't be a page dressed like this, and must be the son of a servant. What she didn't understand was why the High Sheriff didn't even give the boy a pair of shoes to wear. The man must be an ogre to treat his servants this way.

"Thank you," said Maira, dismounting, and handing the boy a coin for his trouble. "Now get in out of the rain before you catch your death of cold."

"Aye, my lady," said the boy hurrying to the stable. Branton helped Morag dismount and led their horses to the stable as well.

"I'll bring your trunks inside as soon as I finish with the horses," Branton called back over his shoulder. He didn't let the rain bother him and continued with his duties no matter what the conditions. Branton had been sent to look after the girls and that is exactly what he did. Maira felt bad now, telling him earlier that he would never be a squire. He was five and ten years of age but had the skills required of a squire and also the demeanor and loyalty involved. Plus, he was good with a blade. Perhaps he would be some knight's squire someday after all.

"Hurry, Maira, let's get in outta the rain." Morag held her hood over her head and ran for the keep. Maira followed.

When she got to the keep, she saw a seasoned man standing in the doorway with his arms crossed and a scowl on his face. He was tall with a round belly. Around him were several guards and behind him stood a nursemaid holding the hand of a toddler.

"Lady Maira, I presume?" the man said to Morag as she approached him. He had dark hair, graying around the temples. A full beard and mustache covered his face. His skin looked weathered and Maira noticed small wrinkles at the corners of his eyes and on his forehead. One cheek had a mole on it that was dark brown and hairy. She flinched inwardly but stayed quiet.

This scoundrel wasn't much of a knight. Instead of venturing into the rain to see to his guests' needs and the needs of a lady, he stood dry inside the keep only worrying about himself. Branton was acting more like a knight than this man was right now.

"Och, I'm no' Lady Maira, I'm Lady Morag," said Morag, lowering the hood of her cape to look at the man who Maira realized was the lord of the castle.

"Too bad. You're a comely one," he said with a grunt. "Why are you here?"

"I came with my cousin at the request of the Earl of Rothbury," Morag explained. "I hope ye dinna mind."

"Where's my betrothed?" he asked, looking out into the pouring rain.

Maira walked up slowly, hood down and with water dripping from her long, strawberry-blond hair. She figured the worse she looked the better the chance the man wouldn't want her for a bride after all. That is exactly what she hoped for. If he despised her, he'd send her back to Rothbury and she wouldn't have to stay a fortnight like her father told her. The quicker she got out of here the better.

"I'm Lady Maira," she said, stepping inside the door to the keep.

The man perused her from head to foot, no expression at all upon his face.

"You're making a puddle on my floor," he complained.

"It's raining, my lord, if you haven't noticed."

"You'll call me High Sheriff like everyone else around here."

"Excuse me, High Sheriff, but I'm cold and wet and would like to retire to my chamber now."

"You're early. Your room isn't prepared yet. Go wait by the fire until I give you word."

"Aye, my lord High Sheriff," she said, using both titles just to spite him. As she walked past him, he called out to stop her.

"Wait! What's that?" he asked.

"What's what?" Maira turned a full circle, looking at the ground, not sure what he meant.

"On your back," he said in a low growl.

"Oh, this." She unsheathed her sword and held it in front of her.

Instantly, the guards standing by the man drew their swords.

"It's my sword," she told him.

"A wench with a sword?" Sir Gregory spat on the ground at her feet. "I won't allow my betrothed to walk around sporting a weapon. Take the blade," he commanded one of his men with a quick jerk of his head.

"My sword stays with me," she told him in a firm and steady voice. "It was a gift from my father, one of the

Legendary Bastards of the Crown. I'm sure you wouldn't want me to tell him you took it away from me, would you?" Maira raised her other hand to stop her blade from being taken away.

The High Sheriff seemed to consider her words. "I don't want to see you wearing that again. Do you understand?"

"Oh, so then you won't want me wearing these either?" She moved aside her cloak to show him the display of daggers attached to her waist belt.

"Egads," growled the man. "You are nothing like a lady. Why wasn't I told this ahead of time?"

"If I'm not a lady to your liking, then perhaps you'd like to find another to wed. I'll collect my things and be on my way immediately."

"Nay. The earl and your father have made an alliance with me and you'll not be going anywhere," said the man. His eyes fell to her waist and his face froze. "Where did you get that jeweled dagger?" He took two steps toward her and reached out for it, but she covered the hilt of it with her hand and stepped back.

"It's mine," she answered. "I got it . . . from a friend."

"That's a lie," he grunted. "That dagger used to be my wife's."

"I don't know who you mean and I assure you the blade is mine."

"Lady Catherine was my wife. She died six months ago."

"Oh. I'm sorry to hear of her passing, High Sheriff. But once again, this couldn't be her dagger, because it's mine."

"It was stolen from her years ago. I never thought I'd see it again."

"I could use a cup of warm, mulled spiced cider and so

could my cousin," said Maira, trying to take attention away from her dagger. "We would like to warm up at the fire." Maira took Morag by the arm and led her to the great hall.

"Maira, ye walked away before we were dismissed," whispered Morag as they entered the great hall and headed over to the fire.

"I don't care." Maira reached over her shoulder and sheathed her sword as she walked. "I told you, I don't want to marry the man so I am not going to listen to a word he says."

"Nay, put that down," came the High Sheriff's bellow.

Maira turned around to see the woman and the toddler standing by the High Sheriff. The little boy had something in his hand and was bringing it to his mouth.

"You'll not put the rushes in your mouth again." The High Sheriff reached out and slapped the boy's hand and then spanked him. The little boy wailed loudly, which only earned him another spanking from the lord of the castle.

"Wait here, Morag," said Maira, hurrying across the great hall and stopping right in front of them. "Do not hurt that boy again," she told Sir Gregory.

The look of surprise on his face told her he was appalled by her action. "You will not tell me how to treat my son," snapped the High Sheriff.

"Your son?" Maira asked, surprised to hear this. A man like him didn't deserve children, and especially not a little boy as cute as this one. "No one told me I was to be a stepmother. I would like to get to know the boy." While Maira didn't plan on marrying the man, if she pretended like she was going to, she might be able to protect the child.

"It's all right," she told the boy, getting down on her knees and holding him to her chest. She rubbed his back as he cried into her wet clothes.

"Get up," commanded Sir Gregory. "You are making a spectacle of yourself. Nursemaid, take the boy above stairs and put him to bed without any dinner."

"Aye, High Sheriff," said the woman, holding out her arms for the boy. Maira didn't want to let the child go. Something inside her made her want to protect him although she had no ties to him at all. But then she saw the fear in the nursemaid's eyes. While Maira didn't want the boy to be punished, neither did she want the servant to suffer for her interference. She released the boy and got to her feet. With a slight nod of her head she told the woman to take him.

"You'll not interfere with the discipline of my son again." Sir Gregory took her by the arm tightly and headed toward the fire in the great hall.

"I don't feel as if the boy deserved a slap and a spanking just for putting the rushes in his mouth."

"I don't care what you think. I will not let a stranger interfere with how I raise my son."

"Stranger?" she asked, feeling her blood boil. "If we're to be married, then that would make the boy my stepson."

"Perhaps so, but that doesn't change a thing. I'll not have a boy who cannot obey my orders."

"I can't sit by and watch a defenseless child be hurt by the hand of a full grown man."

His eyes bore fire and she knew she'd angered him even more. "Page, escort Ladies Maira and Morag to their chamber," called out the man.

"I thought it wasn't yet prepared," she answered snidely.

"I will not be questioned again. Now, you'll go to your

chamber and no food will be sent tonight. Tomorrow, perhaps, you'll see things differently and learn your place as my betrothed."

Tomorrow, Maira thought, she would be long gone from here if she could help it.

Once inside their chamber, Maira closed the door and then rushed over and looked out the open window. It continued to rain. This wasn't going to make her escape easy.

"Maira, that man is horrible," said Morag. "What are we goin' to do?"

"We need to get out of here as soon as possible."

"How are we goin' to do that?"

"I don't know." She paced back and forth. The guards from Rothbury who escorted them there were already gone. Nightfall was upon them and the storm continued to grow worse. Rain blew in gusts through the window so Maira closed the shutter and turned around. Morag sat on the edge of the bed hugging her arms around her. Her cloak and hair were dripping wet and her teeth chattered.

"You're cold and wet," said Maira, ignoring the fact that she was too. She hurried over to the hearth and lit a fire. "Take off that wet cloak and come warm yourself," she instructed.

"Maira, I'm so tired and hungry," said Morag. "I want to go back to Rothbury. Nay, I want to go home to Scotland and be with Fia and the bairn, and with my family."

"I know, Morag. I don't like it here either."

Morag wasn't as strong as Maira and started to cry. "The High Sheriff is angry with ye, but yet he is punishin' me as well. What are we goin' to do?"

Maira's brash actions had caused trouble for Morag. It was

something she never meant to happen. One night of being cold and wet and hungry wasn't something that would break Maira. But Morag needed to be cared for and Maira knew now that she shouldn't have come on so strong with the High Sheriff so quickly.

"I'm sorry about this, Morag. And you are right that you shouldn't be punished for something I did. You stay here. Branton will arrive with our trunks soon. When he does, change into warm clothes and get into bed. I'll be back."

"Maira, dinna leave me," said Morag, wiping a tear from her eye.

"I'm going to sneak down to the kitchen to find us some food. I promise I won't be long."

"Hurry back. And be careful."

"I will." Maira opened the door to find Branton and the young servant boy with the bare feet hauling their trunks to the room.

"Lady Maira, where do you want these?" asked Branton.

"Just put them against the wall inside the room."

"I will. But where are you going?"

"The High Sheriff has already sent us to our chamber with nothing to eat. I am going to sneak down to the kitchen to find some food."

"But if the High Sheriff sees you, he'll be furious," said Branton.

"Then I'll make sure I don't get caught."

"How will ye do that?" asked Morag, coming to the door.

"I don't know. I'm not even sure where to find the kitchen."

"My mother is a cook at the castle," said the young boy. "I can show ya."

"What is your name?" asked Maira.

"I'm Tommy."

"Thank you, Tommy. I would like that. Branton, will you stay here with Morag until I return?"

"I will," said Branton, hauling the trunks into the room. "Will you bring me some food, too? And some wine or ale?"

"Fine," she said, taking to the corridor with Tommy. "How old are you, Tommy?" she asked the boy as they walked.

"I'm nine," he said. "I'm only the son of a servant but hope to someday be a page."

"Where are your shoes?"

"I outgrew my shoes. My mother said my feet are too big for my body."

"Well, why don't you get some bigger shoes?"

"We don't have any money. But now that you gave me this, I am going to save it so someday I can pay a cobbler to make me a pair of shoes." The boy held up the penny she gave him, smiling and showing the missing spaces where he had lost a few teeth.

She spoke in a soft voice as they headed down the corridor. "Why doesn't the High Sheriff give you shoes? He should take care of his servants."

"Before Lord Emery died, we used to have everything we needed. But Lord Gregory is mean and doesn't care about anyone but himself."

"I'm sorry to hear that," said Maira, her heart going out to the boy. "But now that I'm here, I will make sure you have a pair of shoes to wear as well as anything else you need."

"Are you going to be the new Lady of Durham since Lady Catherine died?"

"Well, I don't know about that," she said, not wanting to

reveal to the boy that she had no intention of sticking around that long. "Tell me, where is the kitchen? This castle is so huge that I'm afraid I'm already lost."

"The kitchen is next to the great hall," he told her. "But we can't go that way or the High Sheriff will see you."

"But I need food for my friends."

"There's another way we can go, and no one will see you at all."

"What do you mean?"

"This way," said the boy, leading her down a darkened corridor that looked as if it were a dead end.

"This doesn't lead anywhere," she told him, thinking he was playing a game with her.

"It does, if you know about the secret passageway."

"Secret passage?" She looked around but, in the dark, couldn't see an opening anywhere.

"Under here," he told her, pulling aside a hanging tapestry and pushing against the wall. She heard a creaking noise and then felt a gush of stale air hit her in the face. There was a soft light coming from up ahead. "There's the kitchen," he told her, leading the way.

In the dark, Maira ran her hand against the wall to guide her way. They came upon a maze of openings, and as her eyes became accustomed to the dark, she could see cracks of light every so often.

"What's down these corridors?" she asked, hearing her voice echo in the tunnel.

"They lead all over the castle," the boy told her.

"Does the High Sheriff know about these passageways?" she asked curiously, already devising a plan of escape.

"Nay, my lady. The servants know about them, but no one

has told him, just in case we need a place to hide. Lord Emery never used them and it has only been since the High Sheriff took over the castle that we started using them again."

"Interesting," she said, making a mental note of where to find the entrance to the secret passageway.

The boy pushed aside another tapestry and they entered into the very busy kitchen. None of the servants even paid them any attention as they went about their work. Servants hurried to and fro, baking bread in the large, brick ovens, and turning roasted meat on spits over the open fires. There was a scullery at the far side of the room where the servants washed the dirty dishes in water that they hauled from the well outside.

"My mother is over here. I want you to meet her," said Tommy, taking her hand and pulling her across the room. The servants all looked tired and gaunt and very dirty. She wondered when they'd last washed their clothes or had a bath.

"Mother, this is Lady Maira," said Tommy, stopping in front of a butcherblock table. A tall, thin woman wearing a wimple and a gown covered in flour turned her weary eyes to meet her.

"My lady!" She dropped the dough she was kneading and curtsied. Some of the other servants heard her and stopped what they were doing and bowed and curtsied as well.

"No need for that," she told them with a wave of her hand. "Please, go on and get back to your chores." The last thing she needed was the High Sheriff seeing his servants bowing to her right now.

"Tommy, why did you bring her in here when we're working?" scolded his mother. "If the High Sheriff knows, he will be furious."

"I asked him to," Maira told the woman. "I was hoping to obtain some food for myself as well as my cousin and my page."

"But . . . shouldn't you be sitting at the dais next to the High Sheriff?" asked the woman.

"She's being punished," said Tommy. "Lord Gregory sent her to her chamber without supper, just like he did to Ricker."

"Ricker?" she asked.

"His two-year-old son," said the woman. "Since Lady Catherine died, the boy has been so frightened of Lord Gregory that he stopped talking all together. We're all worried about him."

"That's terrible," said Maira, feeling as if the High Sheriff were a tyrant who needed a good thrashing.

"Servants, what is holding up the meal?" bellowed the High Sheriff from the great hall.

"Quickly, take some food and then you must go," said the woman. She took a basket and filled it with bread and cheese. Then she used a towel to pull a chicken off a spit, wrapping it and putting it into the basket as well. "Tommy, get that bucket of hot cider and a ladle for my lady. And bring a goblet as well."

"Aye, Mother," said the boy, hurrying to do as told.

"Thank you," said Maira, taking the basket from the woman. "What is your name, if I might ask?"

"I am Cleo," she told her, taking the goblet and adding it to the basket. "Tommy, carry the bucket of cider to the room for Lady Maira. Then hurry back and tend to your chores before Sir Gregory notices you are gone."

"Nay, I don't want him to be punished. I'll take it. Thank you," said Maira, taking the bucket from the boy.

"Hurry," said Cleo, looking over her shoulder. "The High Sheriff is heading this way."

Maira took the basket of food and the cider, ducking behind the tapestry and making her way slowly through the darkened tunnel. Not able to see where she was going, she made a wrong turn and ended up getting lost. Seeing a stream of light coming from a hole in the wall, she walked over and looked through it.

"It's someone's bedchamber," she said to herself, realizing this was a peephole. Oftentimes, castles had secret passage-ways and peepholes for the lord of the castle to spy on his guests. That made her wonder if there was a peephole in her room as well.

"Maira? Are ye in there?" came Morag's voice echoing through the tunnel from somewhere up ahead. "Maira, where are ye?"

Maira followed Morag's voice, finding her way out of the darkened maze of tunnels.

"I'm here," she called out, seeing a light up ahead. Branton held back the tapestry while Morag, holding a lit candle, poked her head into the tunnel. "How did you know where to find me?"

"You should know Morag by now," said Branton. "She is too much of a busybody to stay put like you told her. As soon as you left with the boy, she insisted we follow."

"I am no' a busybody, I was just concerned for the safety of my cousin," Morag answered with a sniff.

"It doesn't matter." Maira, for once, was glad that Morag was being curious. "I'm glad you followed or I might have been lost in these dark tunnels for the rest of the night."

"Where do they lead?" Morag stretched her neck to look inside.

"I'm not sure, but they do lead to the kitchen, that much I know. I've got food and hot cider. Let's go back to the room and have something to eat by the fire."

"I'll carry that," said Branton, taking the bucket of cider from her. They made their way back upstairs and were heading to their chamber when, through a closed door, Maira heard a child crying.

"Wait," she said, stopping the others. "I think that sounds like the High Sheriff's young son, Ricker. I want to make sure he is all right."

"Dinna get involved," warned Morag. "The High Sheriff willna like it and might punish us again."

"Aye," added Branton. "He's not a very friendly man. I agree with Morag. Let's go back to the room and eat this food. I'm starved."

"You two go back to the room, but first give me some of the food." She reached into the basket and, using a cloth, pulled a chicken leg off the carcass and wrapped it up. Then she tore off a hunk of bread and picked up the goblet, scooping some hot cider out of the bucket.

"What are ye doin'?" asked Morag.

"I'm taking the poor boy something to eat. He is probably crying because he is hungry. Now go on, I'll meet you back at our chamber."

"But Maira," said Morag, sounding very worried.

"Come on, Morag," Branton told her, taking the basket and bucket both. "Once Lady Maira makes up here mind, there is no stopping her."

They left down the corridor. Maira reached up and

knocked upon the door where she heard the child crying. The boy wailed loudly and the nursemaid tried to calm him. Since they couldn't hear her knocking, Maira pushed open the door and stepped inside the room. The nursemaid looked up in surprise, jumping up from the bed, leaving the little boy laying there, crying.

"My lady," said the woman, wringing her hands in front of her. "I'm sorry, I didn't hear you knock."

"That's all right," Maira told her. "I heard the boy crying and thought he might be hungry, so I brought him some food." She stepped further into the room and closed the door behind her.

"Oh, nay," said the nursemaid, holding out her hands and shaking her head. "The High Sheriff has punished the boy. You can't give him food."

"I don't feel it's right that a two-year-old boy is punished and deprived of food, do you?"

"It is not for me to judge. Please, my lady, you really should go."

"The reason the boy was eating the rushes in the first place is probably because he was hungry, don't you think?"

"I – I – I'm not sure." The woman looked down to the floor when she answered. "The High Sheriff often punishes his son by depriving him of food."

"Well, now that I am here, that is going to change." Maira walked over and sat down on the bed with the food wrapped in the cloth on her lap and the goblet of cider in her hand. "Ricker, Honey, I brought you some food. Are you hungry?"

The little boy stopped crying and sat up wiping his eyes. In the firelight, Maira noticed his beautiful hazel eyes with little

77

specks of green. He had dark hair and a cute little button nose. His gaze fixated on the goblet.

"This is spiced cider," she said, holding out the goblet for him to have a taste. "You must sip it slowly since it is hot."

The boy reached out both hands for the cup. Maira held on to it while the boy took a sip. The corners of his mouth turned up in a smile. Then his eyes dropped to the bundle on her lap. Maira reached out and placed the goblet on a bedside table and proceeded to unwrap the food.

"Do you like chicken?" she asked the young boy.

His eyes lit up and he nodded. She held out the chicken leg and he took it in his little hand and bit into the thick juicy meat. Devouring it hungrily, he looked over for the bread next.

"Here you go," said Maira, handing him the chunk of bread and wiping her hands off on the cloth.

"Lady Maira, you are very kind," said the nursemaid.

"What is your name?" asked Maira.

"I am Teresa," said the woman.

"Why does the High Sheriff treat his son so poorly? He is a noble, and should be spoiled instead of punished. Especially since he is the High Sheriff's heir. Is Ricker his only child?"

"He is," said the woman. "And the High Sheriff didn't use to treat the boy this way while Lady Catherine was alive."

"What happened?" asked Maira curiously.

"Lady Catherine died a few months ago. She had been ill and called for the Bishop of Durham to be at her side. Lady Catherine's father used to invite him to the castle every year on St. Catherine's Day to celebrate. They became friends over the years. The High Sheriff, who was only called Sir Gregory back then, became a friend of Lord Emery's as well as the bishop."

"St. Catherine's Day," repeated Maira, being familiar with the day where women under the age of twenty-five prayed to St. Catherine to find them a husband. "Did their celebrating the feast day have anything to do with the fact Lord Emery's daughter was named Catherine?"

"I think so, my lady. Lady Catherine's late mother was from France where the feast day originated. She didn't want her daughter to be a woman who never married, so they prayed every year to find a good husband for her. It is said that is why they named her Catherine, after the saint."

"And the best husband for her that they could come up with is Sir Gregory?" she asked.

"It isn't my place to say."

"I'm sorry, go on with your story." Maira might have spoken her thoughts aloud and didn't want Teresa to feel uncomfortable by it.

"All I was going to say was that after the bishop's last visit the High Sheriff started acting odd and being mean to his son."

"I wonder why," said Maira.

"No one knows. But little Ricker was so traumatized after the death of his mother that he hasn't spoken a word since. He is also frightened of his own father. I feel bad for the boy, but I have to abide by the lord's orders, my lady. You understand."

"Oh, I understand all too well," said Maira, getting to her feet. "The High Sheriff of Durham is a tyrant, a bully and an ogre. Everyone in the castle seems to be afraid of him, but he isn't going to scare me."

"My lady, please don't tell Lord Gregory you were here

giving food to the boy," said Teresa, her eyes wide with fear. "He will punish all of us for this action."

"My lips are sealed," Maira promised. "I will be leaving in the morning and when I return to Rothbury, I'll send word to my father and let him know about the conditions here. Hopefully, he will be able to do something to help all of you."

"Leaving? But you are the High Sheriff's betrothed, are you not?"

"Not anymore. My father and my guardian might have made the alliance for me, but I have been granted permission by my late grandfather, King Edward III, to choose which man I will marry. And I promise you, it will not be the High Sheriff of Durham.

CHAPTER 6

"**K**eep your elbows bent and close to your body," Jacob instructed one of the village men the next morning. They practiced with the new weapons in the secret camp hidden in the woods just as the sun began to rise. "Nay, Lyle, not like that," Jacob called over his shoulder. He walked over to help another man. "You need a firmer grip on the sword to make it more difficult for your opponent to knock it out of your hand. Like this." He repositioned the man's hands on the hilt.

"Ah, I see," said Lyle. "Thank you, that is much better."

The air was cool and crisp and every time they spoke their breath could be seen. Soon it would be winter and they would have to move deeper into the forest since, without the cover of the leaves on the trees, it would be hard to hide.

"Roger, face your hips toward your opponent and put one foot in front of the other so you have a good base, like this." Jacob demonstrated.

"Aye, I understand, Sir Jacob. Thank ya," said Roger, practicing his stance.

"It's just Jacob now," he reminded the man. "No need to use my title. How many times do I have to remind all of you of that?"

"We'll always think of ya as a knight and nothin' less," said the man. "It is the way we'll remember ya till the day ya die."

"Well, hopefully I, nor any of you, will be dying anytime soon."

Jacob hurried over to where Will was instructing a group of villagers how to use the battle axes they had just obtained.

"Will, can I talk with you?" asked Jacob in a low voice.

"Aye, my lord," said Will, following Jacob over to a clump of bushes.

"We don't have long before the day of the attack."

"Aye," said Will. "I think the villagers will be ready by then. Don't you? They are doing well handling the new weapons."

"That's not what I'm worried about."

"Then what?" asked Will.

"Well, now that I know Lady Maira and her cousin are at Durham Castle, I don't feel as confident about the attack."

"What do you mean, my lord?"

"Dammit, Squire, stop calling me lord. It only hurts too much to hear the title when I am nothing now but a thief."

"Sorry about that. So, what are you planning on doing about Lady Maira?"

"I don't know. I am going to have to find a way to get her and her cousin out of there before the attack." Jacob paced back and forth, feeling very perplexed about the whole thing.

"I have a feeling this has nothing to do with getting your dagger returned," said Will.

"Nay. Not really. You see, ever since I kissed the girl, I have felt something for a woman that I haven't felt since Lady Catherine."

"I see." Will raised a brow. "Could this be that you're still mourning the death of your last lover and that is why you're seeking a replacement?"

"Nay. Aye. Mayhap. I don't know anymore." Jacob ran a weary hand through his long hair. "All I know is that I can't stop thinking about her."

"Catherine?"

"Nay," scowled Jacob. "Maira, you fool. She is like no other lady I have ever met. She seems to have a mind of her own and she is fearless. She can also handle a blade as well as a lot of men I know."

"She sounds as if she'd be an asset to have in our army."

"What did you say?" Jacob's head snapped up.

"I just meant, even though she's a woman, you said yourself that she knows how to handle a blade. But she is inside the castle walls and betrothed to your archenemy. So, I guess that is not an option."

"On the contrary," said Jacob, running a hand over his chin in thought. "She might be exactly what I need to get inside the castle. If luck is on my side, perhaps I can even get her to fight with us."

"Against her betrothed?" asked Will.

"She doesn't want to marry the man. I'm sure of it. This could be our lucky break."

"But what are you going to do? You'd have to get inside the castle to talk to her."

"Then that is what I'll do. I'll wear a disguise, looking like a peasant and hole up near the gates with the beggars. Then when I see her, I'll come up with some excuse to get inside."

"I don't like this. It's too risky." Will frowned. "Why don't you just forget the whole idea?"

"I'm not going to be able to attack if she is in there with her cousin. If anything happens to them, I'll never forgive myself."

"But you don't even know her, my lord."

"Well, I hope to change all that soon."

Jacob looked down the road that led to the castle and wondered how the hell he was going to convince a woman who hated him to be on his side.

* * *

"Morag, hurry up," said Maira, standing watch at the door of their chamber the next morning. "Branton has already taken our trunks to the stable. If we want to get out of here before the High Sheriff awakes, we have to move fast."

Morag yawned and stretched, taking her time putting on her shoes. She wasn't one to awake before the sun, and normally liked to sleep right through the first meal if she could.

"Maira, ye are daft if ye think the High Sheriff is goin' to let us just ride right out the gate. He's goin' to stop us and then we'll be punished again."

"You don't want to stay here, do you?"

"Of course no', ye ken that."

"Then less with the talking and more with the moving. The corridor is empty. Now is our chance." She ran back and took Morag by the hand, pulling her to the door as Morag grabbed her cloak along the way. Then Maira dragged her along as they hurried down the corridor. "If we're quiet, we can sneak past the great hall and out to the stables without anyone seeing us. Put up your hood."

"Aye," said Morag with a yawn, pulling her hood over her head. "What about ye, Maira? Ye should cover yer head, too."

"I WILL."

When Maira lifted her hood over her head, Morag made a face. "Where is yer crown, Maira?"

"Oh, no." Maira's hand flew to her head. "I forgot it in the room. Go to the stable and I'll meet you there. Now hurry!"

Maira rushed back to the room to retrieve her crown that she had placed on the shelf the night before. "I'll not be foolish enough to leave this for the greedy man." After putting the crown on her head, she pulled up her hood and made her way back down the corridor.

Along the way, she had to stop several times and wait in the shadows as some of the High Sheriff's men passed by. Finally, she made it to the courtyard. Rushing into the stable, she found Branton helping Morag up to the bench seat of the wagon. She headed in their direction and was about to call out when she saw the High Sheriff enter the stable.

"And where are you off to so early this morning?" he asked Morag and Branton.

Maira stopped in the shadows and watched, not sure what to do.

"We're goin' . . . out for a ride," said Morag.

"Really?" Sir Gregory made his way to the back of the wagon and peered over the edge. "With your trunks? You were leaving Castle Durham, weren't you?" he asked.

Maira flinched. The man had caught them and if she didn't do something quickly, he was going to punish them again.

"Aye, they are leaving," she said, stepping out to make her presence known.

"Lady Maira?" The man scowled at her. "You were going to leave Castle Durham, too, weren't you? After all, we are betrothed and leaving here would break the alliance. That would be punishable with a spell in the dungeon for both you and your friends."

Maira's eyes met with Morag's and then Branton's. She couldn't let her cousin and Branton be punished because of her actions once again. Nay, she would do whatever she had to in order to protect them. And right now, there was only one thing she could do or say that would allow Branton and Morag to leave unharmed and unpunished.

"Of course not, High Sheriff," she said, forcing a smile. "I was here only to see them off. It seems my cousin has become lonely for her family and so Branton is going to take her home to the Highlands."

"I am?" asked Branton, earning a dirty look from her, willing him to go along with her plan.

"The Highlands?" asked Morag.

Maira shot Morag a look as well that warned her to be quiet. "Dear cousin, it is a long journey home, and I suggest you get going before you end up riding in the dark. That wouldn't be safe."

When the High Sheriff looked the other way, she motioned with her head, and mouthed the words that she would follow later.

"Well, make it a fast goodbye," said Sir Gregory. "I want

you at my side for the morning meal. I'm sure you must be hungry since you had no supper last night."

"Famished," said Maira with another smile and a nod. "I'll be right there as soon as I see my cousin to the gate."

"And take off that damn sword," commanded the High Sheriff as he turned and headed to the great hall.

"Maira, get in the wagon, quickly so we can leave," whispered Morag.

"Aye. I can drive this thing fast enough to get far away before they notice you are gone," added Branton.

"Nay, I can't leave now." Maira looked back toward Sir Gregory and then leaned over and whispered to them. "Go as fast as you can back to Rothbury. Then send a missive to my father right away telling him I am a prisoner here and how awful the High Sheriff really is. If he hears it from you two, he might believe it."

"We're not going anywhere without you, Lady Maira," objected Branton.

"Aye," agreed Morag. "Besides, we have all yer clothes packed on the wagon."

"I don't need them. I won't be here that long. I'm going to try to escape to the woods the first chance I get. I should follow you by only a day or two."

"All right," said Branton, directing the horse from the stable. "If you're sure you don't need me to stay and protect you."

Maira rolled her eyes and drew her sword from her back. "I have all the protection I need right here. Not that you were ever able to protect me, Branton. But I want you to protect Morag now. Promise me that."

"I'll protect Lady Morag with my life," Branton told her

almost a little too enthusiastically. It worried her, but she had no choice. She had to send them away before it was too late.

"Good. Now, I'll walk you to the gate and then ride as fast as you can out of here before the High Sheriff changes his mind and wants you to stay. Whatever you do, don't stop and don't turn back."

Maira sheathed her sword and walked with the wagon, stopping at the front gate as Branton and Morag left her there alone. Morag turned back with tears in her eyes, making Maira want to run and jump in the cart to go with them. But she couldn't. It would only endanger Morag and Branton and she wouldn't have that again.

She watched out the gate, looking past the many beggars standing around the entrance who were crying out for food or coin. Then she reached into her pouch and pulled out a coin and handed it to one of the children. All of a sudden, the crowd of beggars all crowded around her, tugging on her gown and holding out their hands.

"Give me a copper, too," shouted an old woman with rotten teeth.

"We want food," said a man, digging his nails into her arm.

"Help us," shouted someone else as they came at her like a swarm of angry bees.

She stepped back and stumbled, falling on the ground. With her sword on her back and with all the daggers attached to her waist belt it became impossible to get up with the crowd hovering over her.

"Get back," shouted one of the beggars, pushing the others away. The man stood between her and the others with his arms outstretched, keeping them at bay. When the crowd subsided, he turned around and held out his hand to her. "Allow me to help you to your feet, Lady Maira."

"Thank you," she said, taking his strong hand, wondering how the man knew her name since she had just arrived in Durham and didn't even know anyone yet. Then she noticed the leather wrist guards he wore, realizing he was not a beggar at all. She yanked the jeweled dagger from her waist belt and held out the tip to his chest.

"Who are you and what do you want?"

"I'm an old acquaintance of yours, and I want my dagger returned."

"Jacob?" she said in a half-whisper. Her heart sped up a beat as he raised his chin to show her his face. "What are you doing disguised as a beggar?"

"I need to talk to you, Lady Maira."

"Lady Maira," called out a guard, hurrying over to her. "Is this man giving you trouble?"

"Meet me in the forest later, but don't let anyone follow you," he whispered, keeping his eye on the approaching guard.

"What? Nay! Why would I do that?"

"Go west until you see the fork in the road. Then veer off to the left, and head for the thicket and the tallest rowan tree you see."

"Rowan tree?" she asked, thinking of her father since Rowen was his name. She wished he were here to help her right now. If she did what Jacob told her, what was saying the man wouldn't kill her and bury her body in the forest? But if she stayed at the castle, there was no telling the High Sheriff wouldn't kill her when he went off on one of his next rampages.

"Lady Maira," the guard said, approaching her.

"I'll be waiting," whispered Jacob, lowering his head and backing up into the crowd.

"I'm fine," Maira told the guard, her eyes still fastened to Jacob as he disappeared. "They are just poor beggars and you can't blame them for trying." She looked down to the jeweled dagger in her hand, knowing Jacob had probably come to get it. But then, why hadn't he taken it from her? She thought of how the High Sheriff had told her it was once Lady Catherine's dagger. And hadn't one of Jacob's men called him lord?

Suddenly, her curiosity was piqued and she knew without a shadow of a doubt where she would be later today.

CHAPTER 7

The sun was already starting to set and still, Lady Maira had not shown. Jacob held on to his sword, staring out at the woods that led to the road leading to the castle. Most of the villagers had gone back to their homes and there were only a dozen men left that would spend the night and watch over the camp.

"My lord, the roasted pheasant is ready. Do have something to eat," said Will, coming to join him.

"Nay, I'm not hungry." Jacob shoved his sword into the scabbard at his waist.

"She's not coming, is she?"

"I thought for sure she would." Jacob ran his hand through his tangled hair. He had worked hard training his men today, only taking a break to go to the castle. When he saw Maira again, all common sense left his head.

"Well, at least you were able to get your dagger returned, that's the main reason you went there," said Will, gnawing on a piece of meat.

"About that . . . things didn't work out the way I planned."

"You saw her, and yet you walked away without your dagger?" asked Will in confusion. "Oh, she didn't have the blade on her, did she?"

"Clenched in her hand and aimed right at me," he muttered, turning and walking back to the fire. The smell of roasted pheasant filled the air.

"And you let her keep it and then invited her to our secret camp?" asked Will. "I'm not understanding what you were thinking, my lord."

"Hell, I don't know what I was thinking either. Once I saw her, all I wanted was to pull her in my arms again and kiss her and never let her go."

"You are acting . . . quite strange," remarked Will. "Almost like you're lovesick, the way you were with Lady Catherine."

"That's nonsense. I don't even know the girl."

Will looked over Jacob's shoulder and nodded. "Then, this might be the time to change all that. I do believe I see her coming through the woods right now."

Jacob spun around, smiling when he saw the petite woman atop her horse making her way slowly through the brush.

"JACOB?" Maira called out nervously, having snuck out of the castle nearly getting caught by the High Sheriff in the process. She had started having second thoughts when the sun began to set and she found herself lost in the forest looking for the thief. Then she heard voices and saw the rowan tree and headed in that direction. This could be the biggest mistake of her life. How she wished she had her cousins at her side right now. This wasn't the same as sneaking out of Castle Rothbury and to Imanie's secret garden. Now, Maira was in a strange place and all alone. Every decision she made could cost her her life.

"Lady Maira." Jacob rushed over to greet her with the young man who had called him lord right behind him. "I didn't think you were going to show."

Maira surveyed the area from atop her horse. There was a fire with roasted meat on a spit, and tents dotting the small clearing. Half a dozen men looked up, sitting on the ground eating their meal and drinking from bottles. She wasn't sure just what she'd rode into the middle of, or if she should turn right around and leave.

"Come, let me help you dismount." He raised his hands to her but she hesitated. Was this some sort of trap? What would happen to her if she got off the horse? She would be vulnerable and unable to flee on foot.

"I'm not sure," she said, weighing out the options.

"Trust me." He continued to hold out his hands for her.

"Trust you? You're a thief."

"But he's a good thief," said the other man with a smile.

"You. I saw you in the armory," she said with a nod of her head, still holding tightly to the reins of the horse getting ready for a fast escape. "You were one of them who stole weapons from Castle Rothbury.

"Aye, that's me," said the young man with a proud smile. "My name is Will. So glad to finally meet you, Lady Maira. I've heard so much about you."

"Really." Her eyes darted over to Jacob. "And what did you hear?"

"Lady Maira, perhaps we can finish this conversation over a mug of ale and some roasted pheasant."

The food smelled good and Maira was very hungry. She had faked being ill and left the meal in the great hall early in order to sneak away. "Mayhap, I'll stay just for a moment. But don't anyone get any ideas because I've got my weapons and I'm not afraid to use them."

"Nay, you're not. I can vouch for that," said Jacob with a chuckle. "Now let me help you dismount."

"I don't need help," she protested. But before she could object again, Jacob's large hands enclosed around her waist and he lifted her off the horse. Her hands went out to steady herself, holding on to his strong, wide shoulders. When he lowered her to the ground, she was so close to him that she smelled the leather of his arm guards and could see his dark lashes and the slight sunken indention under his eyes. He looked drawn and tired.

"What is this place?" she asked, stepping away from him and surveying the camp.

"It's a hidden camp, not unlike that secret garden of yours," he told her. "We move a lot so as not to be discovered by the castle guards."

"That secret garden wasn't mine, but it was at one time my mentor's. And why are you hiding out here? Is it because you are a thief?"

"It's so much more than that, my lady. You see, I have been training villagers and commoners to fight. That is why I needed the weapons."

"Fight?" she asked in surprise. "Against who?"

"The High Sheriff," Jacob told her, causing her to gasp.

"Do you think you should be telling her that?" asked Will under his breath.

"I don't believe Lady Maira holds any love for the High Sheriff even if she is betrothed to him. After all, everyone hates the man."

"That's right, even Lady Catherine didn't like him and she was his wife."

"Leave us," Jacob told Will. "All of you, leave us," he called out to the men. The others who were gathered around the fire mumbled amongst themselves. Gradually, one by one, they took their food and ale and made their way into the tents or the woods, vacating the area around the fire and leaving Jacob alone with Maira. "Come," said Jacob, guiding her with his warm hand on the small of her back toward the fire. The night was cool and she felt chilled. Sitting in front of a hot fire with a bite of food was just what she needed.

Once they were settled, Jacob handed her a metal plate with roasted pheasant on it. Then he poured some ale into a wooden goblet and handed her that as well.

"Thank you," she said, eagerly consuming the food. "Aren't you going to have any?" She looked up and eyed him suspiciously. "This isn't poisoned, is it?"

That made him laugh. "Why would I want to poison you?"

"To get your dagger back."

"If I wanted to take my dagger, I would have done so by now. And I wouldn't have to kill you to take it."

"I see." She put down the bones and wiped her hands on a cloth he'd given her, not wanting to take any more chances until she knew what was going on. "Who are you?" she asked bluntly.

"I'm nobody."

"What happened to make you live like this? As a thief?"

"The High Sheriff of Durham happened."

She cocked her head, listening intently. "Go on."

"I didn't invite you here for pity and I don't have time to explain."

"Then why did you ask me here?"

"I want you to fight with me. In my army. We're going to attack and seize Durham Castle soon."

"Attack? Do you mean to kill my betrothed?"

"Aye, I will kill him if I have to."

"And you have the crazy notion that I am going to help you do this? You are insane!" She jumped to her feet, wanting to leave. "Why would you even tell me this? Aren't you afraid I'll run back and tell Sir Gregory?"

"Don't take me for a fool, my lady. I know the man too well. And from what little I've seen from you, I am sure you would never want to spend the rest of your life married to someone like him."

"You presume an awful lot. You know nothing about me, so don't pretend you do."

"I know you walk around with enough weapons on you for three men and you also want more than anything to use them. Do you think the High Sheriff would let you do that?"

"Nay. He already threatened me and told me to put them away."

"Don't forget, I was also standing outside the gate when you sent your cousin and that page to safety."

"They were just going out for a ride."

"With your trunks in the cart? Don't lie to me, Maira. They were escaping the High Sheriff and you will be doing the same thing next."

How did this man know so much about her when she knew so little about him? She wanted to stay and find out more, but night was closing in fast. Then she heard the bell ringing from the tower of Durham Castle and knew they had discovered she was missing.

"They're looking for me," she said, turning and heading back to her horse. "I must return to the castle at once."

"Stay," he said, grabbing her by the arm. She stopped and turned and looked up into his steely gray eyes. She saw desperation as well as compassion in his gaze. His outward appearance said he was strong but she saw vulnerability within him. She caught him looking at her lips again. Then, before she knew it, he dipped down and covered her mouth with his. Her head told her to deny him but her heart beat quickly, telling her to trust him. Aye, she wanted to stay with him instead of going back to the High Sheriff – the man she despised. But staying here in the woods with the thief was much too dangerous.

"I can't," she said, not at all sounding sure of herself and he was apt to notice.

"I could use someone as skilled with a blade as you to help finish training my army."

"I don't understand. You – you *want* me to fight?" she asked, just to make sure. "You are urging me to use my weapons?"

"Isn't that what you want more than anything? Even more than marrying a man?"

"I'm not sure," she said, suddenly feeling very confused.

"Don't go back to him, Maira. Please. I know him too well. He will control you and take everything from you that you love. If you marry him, you will be miserable. You will become his puppet and give up everything that makes you feel alive."

Was he speaking the truth? Maira had no doubt he was. But yet, she couldn't stay here. She didn't belong here. And her father would be furious if he knew she was even considering joining this man's army and plotting to kill the exact man that she was sent to marry to make an alliance.

"You never told me why you are doing this," she said, needing to know more before she made the decision.

"Stay, and I'll tell you everything you want to know."

The bell rang out louder, and with it her nerves rattled. She wasn't looking forward to having to answer to the High Sheriff. If she stayed here, she would never have to marry him or answer to him again. But if she didn't return, what would happen to that innocent little sweet boy named Ricker? She kept hearing the child cry in her mind, and kept seeing not only his frightened eyes, but also those of the nursemaid and Cleo and little Tommy without any shoes.

"I'll think about it," she said, quickly mounting her horse. Then with one last glance at Jacob, she turned and rode like the devil back to the castle, wondering what lie she would tell the High Sheriff to keep him from punishing her or from searching the forest. The last thing she wanted was to reveal the secret hiding place of Jacob and his men.

"WHAT DID SHE SAY, MY LORD?" asked Will, hurrying to Jacob's side.

"She said she'll think about it." Jacob kicked at the dirt. "I thought I could convince her to stay, but it didn't work. I need more time."

"Is that why you kissed her?" asked Will.

"Nay. I kissed her because I wanted her to know that I cared about her and that she could trust me. I want her to choose me instead of the High Sheriff. God's eyes, Will, if she doesn't come back I don't know what I'm going to do. I can't allow that man to take anything else from me. I swear I will do anything I have to so that will never happen again."

CHAPTER 8

*B*y the time Maira got back to the castle, she was feeling very shaken. She had met Jacob in the woods like he'd asked, but she'd never expected to find out he was training an army to kill the High Sheriff and take the castle as his own. No matter how rotten Sir Gregory was, did he deserve to die? She didn't think so. Or at least not until she rode through the castle gate and realized the bell wasn't tolling to warn that she had escaped. Nay, the bell tolled for someone else altogether.

"Bring that escaped servant here," she heard Sir Gregory call out.

Not even being noticed because of all the commotion, Maira dismounted and gave the reins of her horse to a stable-boy. "What is happening?" she asked.

"The High Sheriff caught one of the servants sneaking out the castle gate after sunset," the boy relayed the information. "No servant is allowed to leave, and anyone caught doing so is punished severely."

"Oh, that's unfortunate," she said, already feeling bad for

the servant. "What will the High Sheriff do to him?"

"Normally, he'd whip the servant and throw them into the dungeon for a fortnight with little food or water. But because the boy is so young, he might put him in the pillory and have everyone throw rotten food at him instead."

"Young? How young? Who is the servant boy who tried to escape?"

"His name is Tommy and he is nine years old. He is a good friend of mine and I'm frightened for his safety."

"Tommy?" Her heart lodged in her throat. "The son of Cleo, the cook?"

"Aye, that's him. I tried to stop him from leaving but he saw you ride out, my lady. He was very upset and didn't want you to go."

"He was going after me?"

"Aye, he was."

"What is your name?" she asked the boy.

"I'm Alfred, my lady. But all my friends call me Alf."

"Tell me, Alf, does anyone else know I left?"

"I don't believe so. Tommy is loyal and I'm sure he won't tell the High Sheriff why he was leaving the castle walls. He won't divulge your secret."

"If he won't, then I will," she answered, determined to set the record straight. She started to leave the stable when the boy stopped her.

"My lady, I know I am out of line to speak so boldly. But I see your sword strapped to your back and all your daggers at your waist."

"Aye, those are my weapons. I don't go anywhere without them."

"But . . . didn't the High Sheriff warn you not to wear them?"

"Aye, he did. But that doesn't mean anything to me."

"I'm afraid he might take them away from you, or punish you again, my lady."

"Oh. I suppose you're right." Maira weighed the consequences in her mind. If she were going to have any chance of helping poor Tommy, it wouldn't be wise to anger the man any more than she already had. "Do me a favor, Alf." She hurriedly removed her sword and daggers.

"Anything for you."

"I need you to keep my weapons here for now." She looked up to the loft that held hay. "Hide them in the hayloft so I'll know where they are if I need them. But tell no one about it. Do you understand?"

"I do, my lady. It'll be our secret." He collected up her weapons and she handed him a coin for his trouble.

"Nay, I can't take your money," said the boy.

"But I want to do something to show you my gratitude."

"Then help Tommy," he said. "And stay at Durham Castle and help the rest of the servants as well."

"It sounds as if no one likes the High Sheriff." She slipped the coin back inside her pouch.

"He is an awful man and treats not only the servants but also the serfs and villagers terribly. When Lady Catherine was alive she would help us behind his back. But now that she's gone, we have no one."

"That's not true," said Maira, wanting more than anything to protect these poor people. "You have me. You can count on me now. Tell the others I will do whatever it takes to help them in any way possible."

"Thank you, my lady. I only wish there was a way to do that without you having to marry the man."

"Mayhap there is," she said, thinking of Jacob and his request for her to join his army. She headed out to the courtyard, pushing her way to the front of the crowd. There were torches lit and placed in a circle. And in the center of the circle was Tommy locked in the pillory. Only his head and hands stuck out.

"Guards, pass out the rancid scraps of food," called out Sir Gregory. "Everyone, throw it hard at the boy to teach him a lesson."

"But that's my son," shouted Cleo. "Don't anyone hurt him. Please." Cleo pushed to the front of the crowd but one of the guards shoved her and she fell to the ground.

"Delbert, lock her in the pillory as well," Sir Gregory said to his right hand man.

"Aye, my lord," said Delbert, stomping over to Cleo and gripping her by the arm.

"Nay! Leave her alone." Maira hurried forward, falling to her knees, cradling Cleo's head against her. "This woman has done nothing wrong. She is only trying to protect her son like any good parent would do."

"Where have you been?" snapped the High Sheriff. "You are my betrothed and need to be at my side at all times."

"All times but when you decide to lock me in my chamber without any food?" she asked, helping Cleo to her feet. Mumbles went up from the crowd for the way she spoke so boldly to the man. "Tommy is innocent," she told him.

"My guards found him sneaking out of the castle," growled the High Sheriff. "He's a runaway servant and will be punished for his action."

"Nay. He was coming after me and that is the only reason he left the castle."

"What?" asked the High Sheriff. "Where were you?"

"I went out for a ride," she told him. "I didn't know I wasn't allowed to leave. The boy was coming after me to warn me."

"Is that true?" The High Sheriff turned back to Tommy. His frightened little body shook and his eyes darted over to Maira. The guard let go of Cleo. Maira walked forward to hold one of Tommy's hands.

"Of course, it's true," she said. "Do you really think the boy was running away when his mother was still at the castle? How far do you think he would have gotten when you won't even give him a pair of shoes to wear?"

"That's true, he doesn't have shoes," came a voice from the crowd.

"He only has a thin, ripped tunic and worn out breeches," said someone else.

"None of us have what we need," said another voice from the crowd.

"It wasn't this way when Lady Catherine was alive," said a man.

"Silence! All of you," shouted Sir Gregory. Then he turned and glared at Maira. "How do I know you weren't trying to leave me? Perhaps you were the one running away, not the servant."

"Me?" she asked and faked a chuckle. "I was merely going out for a ride in the fresh night air like I always used to do at Rothbury. If I were leaving for good, don't you think I'd have my weapons with me? Do you see them on me?" She held out the sides of her cloak and even turned around to show him it was so. "Besides, you are my betrothed," she added, feeling sickened by what she was going to say next. "I would never leave the man I am to marry. I am to be your wife soon. Why on earth would I leave?"

She held her breath, hoping she'd sounded convincing enough that the High Sheriff believed her. If not, she wasn't sure what she would do to help Tommy and Cleo.

"Release the boy," ordered Sir Gregory. "And let the woman go as well. But let this be a lesson to you to all that I will not tolerate my rules being broken. Next time, I won't be so lenient, no matter what the reason is that someone leaves these walls without permission. Now everyone, back to work."

Maira released a breath of relief as the guards opened the pillory and Tommy ran into his mother's arms. From across the courtyard, Maira spotted the nursemaid holding little Ricker. The boy had his face buried against the woman's chest.

Maira's heart broke that the poor little boy had to witness his own father doing such horrible things. Ricker was only two, but would the High Sheriff raise him to follow in his footsteps? This was a very impressionable age. The boy could very well start believing in time that there wasn't anything wrong with being a tyrant just like his father.

When Maira had returned to the castle, she had every intention of warning the High Sheriff that there was an army hiding in the woods getting ready to attack and kill him. But now, she wasn't so sure that warning him was the right thing to do. She had a lot to think about and many decisions to make. It had, at first, seemed so easy just to walk away and leave Durham Castle, the High Sheriff, and everyone here behind. But now, she knew secrets that could affect everyone, and wasn't sure what to do.

She put her hand on her heart brooch thinking of Imanie and wondering what the old woman would tell her. Maira had never run from trouble or challenges in her life. She had always been the protector of her cousins. But now her cousins weren't here. Should she be protector to the poor servants of Durham instead? And should she join Jacob and his army, finally getting her chance to use her skills with weapons in ways she had always wished she could? Or should she make an alliance with the High Sheriff and marry him the way her father and the earl suggested?

Maira headed up to her chamber to be alone and think. She had some very important decisions to make, and this wasn't going to be easy.

JACOB STOOD outside the castle gates with Will, hidden in the shadows. He'd followed the girl to make certain she returned safely to the castle. Actually, he also followed her to try to find out if she was going to reveal to the High Sheriff all Jacob's plans.

"Did you see that?" whispered Will as they watched Maira bravely take on the High Sheriff.

"Aye," said Jacob softly. "She put her own safety at risk to help those servants."

"Not unlike what you're doing with the villagers," said Will.

"Perhaps," he answered in deep thought. "However, I don't

know what she is going to do. We'll have to keep a close eye on her. She is very unpredictable."

"Do you think she'll come back to the forest and join you, my lord?"

"I don't know. But if she doesn't, I am going to have to convince her somehow, no matter what it takes."

aira tossed and turned that night, unable to sleep, having too much on her mind. She kept going back and forth with her decision, not knowing what to do to remedy the situation.

Finally drifting off to sleep, she found herself in her safe place – Imanie's secret garden.

"Don't be afraid, Maira. You have never feared anything before," came Imanie's voice from the porch of her cottage.

"Imanie?" Maira looked up but everything was foggy. Then the fog cleared and the old woman lunged at her with a sword in her hand. Without thinking, Maira pulled her sword from the scabbard on her back and protected herself from Imanie's blow. "Imanie, what are you doing?" she cried.

"I am here to prove a point. Now put down the sword."

Maira did as told. Imanie lowered her sword as well.

"I don't understand," said Maira.

"You didn't hesitate to protect yourself with your weapon, just as I've taught you."

"Aye, but you didn't warn me you'd be attacking me either."

"It is second nature for you to protect yourself as well as others who are in need."

"I suppose so," agreed Maira.

"Fighting is your skill, Maira. And although your strength is physical, sometimes you might have to find your strength without using your weapons."

Maira didn't know any other way to be strong. "How can I do that?"

"You already have. Didn't you help Cleo and Tommy without using your weapons?"

"Well, yes, but –"

"And little Ricker as well? These people need a strong woman such as you to lead them. Don't abandon them and let them down."

"I know you're right, Imanie. But now Jacob wants me to join his army and fight against the High Sheriff."

"Will you?"

"Nay! How could I? Jacob is a thief and wants to steal Durham Castle and kill my betrothed."

Imanie laughed heartily, unnerving Maira.

"Why are you laughing at me?" she asked her mentor.

"I'm laughing at the way you fool yourself," answered Imanie.

"How so?"

"I am spirit, Maira. I might not be here in the physical state anymore, but I still watch over you girls from beyond the grave. We both know you won't marry the High Sheriff. Not only because of who he is and what he does, but because you have fallen for another man."

"I haven't," she protested. "I don't want to marry anyone!"

"What about the thief?"

"What about him?" she asked.

"You have feelings for him."

"He is naught but a thief! I would never marry a commoner – if I ever decided to marry at all."

"Everyone has their secrets, my lady. And Sir Jacob Quincey has many secrets that he's yet to reveal to you."

"Sir? Are you saying he is a noble? I don't understand."

"Didn't you hear his squire call him, my lord?"

"His squire? Do you mean Will? Imanie, tell me what you know."

"I know that you, my dear, need to listen to your heart more and less to your head. Then you will know exactly what to do."

Maira awoke to a soft knocking at her door. With the reflexes of a trained warrior, she jumped out of bed, reaching for her weapons that were no longer there.

"Who's there?" she called out, hurrying over to dress as quickly as she could.

"It's Tommy," came a muffled voice from the other side of the door.

"Tommy?" she asked, pulling her gown over her head and rushing over to let him in. The little boy stood there with a candle in his hand. The corridor was dark since it was early morning and the sun had not yet risen.

"Tommy? What are you doing here?" she whispered, scanning the corridor quickly.

"Follow me, my lady," said the boy.

"Wait." She ran back and slipped into her shoes, then took her crown from the bedside table and placed it on her head. She didn't want to leave it behind because she wasn't sure she could trust that the High Sheriff wouldn't want to take that from her next. "Where are we going?"

"Alf has someone in the stable who wants to meet with you in secret. I suggest we take the secret passageway so we don't alert anyone."

"Who is it that wants to meet with me?" she asked.

"He didn't say. But he did say to hurry. And thank you, Lady Maira, for coming to my aid when the High Sheriff threw me in the pillory."

"I would do anything to help you, Tommy, but you need to promise me that you won't follow me again."

The boy stopped at the entrance to the tunnel and looked up to her with wide eyes. The light from the candle threw shadows upon him.

"Please, don't leave us again, Lady Maira. We need you. We will die without you."

She took a minute to digest his words, feeling the need in her heart to be here for Tommy and the others, just like Imanie told her. "I am not going to abandon you or the others. I promise." She laid her hand on his shoulder to comfort him. "Now take me to the stable so I can meet this mysterious stranger."

* * *

JACOB PACED BACK and forth in the stable, keeping his eye on the horizon. He was lucky enough to have been able to swim the moat and climb the wall to get inside. He could have taken one of the secret tunnels, but it looked as if the guards were too near and he didn't want to chance that they would see him. Having lived at this castle for ten long years, he knew every way possible to sneak in or out. He sincerely doubted the High Sheriff knew about the secret passageways because no one who knew would be willing to tell him.

Jacob needed to get out of here before the sun rose or he

might not be as lucky to leave without the High Sheriff catching him.

"Here they come," said Alf, leaning on the door to the stable, watching in the dark for Tommy to return with Maira. Jacob felt his throat tighten and there was a churning in his gut as well. What if Maira didn't want him here? If she called out to the guards when she saw him, he would be imprisoned and would never have the chance to lead the attack. This was all a huge risk and he hoped he read her right, but it was a chance he felt he just had to take.

"Alf, who is it?" asked Maira when she entered the stable. "Is someone here to see me?"

"Aye, it's me, my lady." Jacob stepped out of the darkness and into the light of a lantern hanging from a hook. He lowered his hood to let her see his face.

"Jacob!" she said in surprise, her beautiful blue eyes opening wide. Her brows raised and then lowered in an inquisitive manner "Why are you here?"

"I had to see you again," he admitted, hoping not to be turned away.

"Sir Jacob said it was important, or I wouldn't have sent Tommy to fetch you," Alf broke in.

"Hello, Sir Jacob," said Tommy with a smile.

"Hello, Tommy," answered Jacob, happy to see the boy again. "You have grown much since I last saw you." Jacob reached out and ruffled the boy's hair. Tommy smiled shyly and looked to the ground.

Maira's eyes shot over to the boys. "Tommy? Alf? How do you boys know Jacob?"

"Sir Jacob lived here at one time," explained Alf.

"He was the late Lord Durham's Captain of the Guard,"

said Tommy. "I was only five when he left, but I'll never forget how kind he was to me and how he even took me for a ride atop his horse once. Everyone loved him."

"We miss you, Sir Jacob," said Alf. "It's not the same here without you."

"I miss you boys, too," said Jacob. "Now, will you two keep watch and let us know if anyone comes?"

"Aye, my lord," said Alf, going to the door along with Tommy as lookouts.

"You shouldn't have come," Maira whispered.

"I wasn't sure if you'd return to see me again in the woods. I didn't want to take the chance that you wouldn't."

"Let's talk up there," said Maira, motioning with her head to the hayloft.

"All right," he said, curiously, wondering why she would suggest being alone with him.

They climbed to the hayloft together. Jacob stood right behind her and held on to the ladder, blocking her body with his so she wouldn't fall. Once they reached the top, Maira pulled him to her forcefully and covered his mouth with hers. Now he understood why she wanted him up here in private. She didn't want the boys to witness their kiss.

"That's nice," he whispered, pulling back and running his fingers lightly over her jawline. "I must say I didn't expect it. Why did you do it?"

"It is my way of apologizing."

"For what?"

"For this." Then she did something else that surprised him. She reached out and slapped him hard across the cheek.

Jacob took a minute to try to figure out what had just

113

happened, not understanding any of it. "Why did you kiss me if you were only going to slap me afterwards?"

Her face was in shadow, but he could still see her scowl from the light of the lantern filtering up through the slats in the floor.

"Why didn't you tell me you once lived at Durham Castle and were Captain of the Guard? You failed to mention you are a noble."

"You didn't ask," he told her with a lopsided grin. "Besides, it doesn't matter. I no longer hold a title thanks to the High Sheriff."

"What happened?" she asked, sounding as if she were truly concerned.

"He framed me for the death of a bishop," Jacob told her. "And then he had the pope excommunicate me."

"Oh, that's awful."

"Maira, he took from me not only my title, but my chance of being High Sheriff, not to mention the Lord of Durham someday."

"You? Why would you be lord of the castle or High Sheriff?"

"Because," he answered, not wanting to tell her everything. "Let's just say this all would have been mine but thanks to your betrothed, I am naught but an outcast. I live the life of a thief in the night, always hiding for fear of being found and slain."

"And that is why you want your revenge?"

"Isn't it enough?"

"I don't know. Planning on attacking and killing a man and seizing his castle – that doesn't make you any better than Sir Gregory, does it?"

"Either you're for me or against me," he growled, not having patience for this right now. "Which is it?"

She took a minute, and then she nodded and dug her dagger out from under the hay. "I'll help you however I can, but I won't fight for or against you. My weapons are only to protect those I feel are in danger." She dug her sword out next and strapped it on her back.

"I could use someone like you who is skilled with a blade. I want you to help me finish training my army. Will you do it?"

"Me?" The tone of her voice told him she was honored but, at the same time, hesitant to agree. "I can't get away from the castle without Sir Gregory knowing about it. He has ordered that I stay at his side at all times. I'm afraid it would be impossible."

"Sneak out the tunnels at night, and come to the woods," he told her. "The boys can show you how to get in and out without being seen."

"There's a tunnel that leads to the woods and yet you look as if you swam the moat?"

"I like a challenge," he told her, reaching down to kiss her once again.

"You're wet," she said, pushing him away. "Next time, use the tunnel if you want to get close to me."

"Next time?" he asked, thinking this sounded promising.

"Lady Maira, Lord Jacob, someone's coming," whispered Tommy from the bottom of the ladder.

"I have to go," whispered Jacob, looking down into the stable. "Promise me you'll come see me again." Jacob didn't wait for her answer. He kissed her once again and then grabbed a rope on a pulley that was hanging from the ceiling.

In one fluid movement, he used it as support as he swung out the window and left Maira standing there alone.

"Jacob! Nay!" cried Maira running to the window. She clutched the sill tightly and frantically looked down, afraid he had hurt himself with the fall. But when she saw his shadow as he ran toward the back wall, she realized he would be all right.

"Hurry, my lady," called Tommy.

"I'm coming," she said, fastening the rest of her weapons to her waist belt and hurrying down the ladder.

"It's all right. It's just the guards at the watch tower switching posts," announced Alf from the door.

"Either way, I need to get back to my chamber before Sir Gregory discovers I'm gone." Maira followed Tommy through the shadows, noticing the sun starting to light up the horizon. When they got to the entrance of the tunnel that was inside the mews, two guards were talking right outside the door. There was a hidden opening that led into the courtyard from the keep. It was inside the mews that butted up to the main structure. The opening was small and at the back of the dark area where the birds were kept. No one who didn't know it was there would ever notice it.

"Now we're doomed," said Maira as they watched from behind a wagon.

"Nay, we're not," said Tommy. "There's another way in, but you might get wet."

"I don't mind," she said. "Where is it?"

They made their way to the well and Tommy started to climb over the edge.

"Wait, what are you doing?" she asked.

"Once you drop into the well, there is a hole part way up. It leads right into the tunnels."

Maira looked down into the well not wanting to drop into the water with her weapons, and not wanting to have to go back to the hayloft to hide them again.

"I have a better idea," she said. "All we have to do is cause some kind of distraction to take the guards' attention. Then we can sneak into the tunnel the usual way."

"I think Alf is already ahead of us on that. Look." Tommy smiled and pointed across the courtyard over toward the barn. She saw Alf letting the huge sow out of her pen. Then he rushed over and opened the door to the kennels. Two dogs rushed out chasing the squealing pig that took off across the courtyard. A moment later, both guards ran after it enabling Maira and Tommy to sneak in through the mews in the usual way.

Maira and Tommy laughed as they hurried through the tunnels in the dark. Maira lived for excitement. Being on the edge of danger made her blood pump wildly through her body. She supposed she got that from her father who was once a pirate.

"I can make it on my own from here, Tommy," Maira told him when they got to the bend in the tunnel that led to the kitchen. "You go to the kitchen immediately and mention this to no one."

"Thank you, Lady Maira. I consider you a good friend."

Maira made her way to the hidden exit and pulled back the tapestry, scanning the darkened corridor. Satisfied no one would see her, she hurried to her room feeling invigorated from the excitement and alive from Jacob's kiss.

Now that her dream with Imanie was verified that he had once been a titled man, it made her anxious to help him retrieve his standings. But being excommunicated by the pope, not to mention murdering a bishop, were serious offenses. Even if Jacob had been framed, he would have to find a way to prove it and convince the pope to reverse the charges. It would be nearly impossible. Her heart ached for Jacob because no man should have to suffer the way he had for something he didn't even do.

She pushed open the door to her room, feeling jubilant that she hadn't been caught. A smile lit up her face but soon disappeared when she saw the High Sheriff lounging back on her bed with his hands behind his head.

"Hello, Lady Maira," he said snidely. "How nice of you to finally arrive. Now, why don't you tell me just where you've been?"

CHAPTER 10

*S*ir Gregory Arundell was the last person in the world that Maira wanted to see right now. Especially in her bed!

"My lord," she said in surprise, not knowing why he was there or what he wanted.

"I came to escort you to the great hall for the meal," he drawled. "When there was no answer at the door, I entered to find you were missing again."

"I didn't leave the castle walls, honest, I didn't," she told him, not wanting to be punished again. "I just went out for a walk in the courtyard to see the sunrise."

"Really? It's funny none of my men saw you there." He slid off the bed and that's when she noticed his sword attached to his waist belt. He noticed she wore hers as well. "Is it common for you to walk for pleasure inside the security of the castle walls saddled down with weapons I told you not to wear again?"

"I always wear my weapons. They were given to me by my father and make me feel comforted."

"We both know damned well that the jeweled dagger was not given to you by your father. That belonged to my wife, Lady Catherine. It was stolen years ago and I think I know who did it." He stepped closer to her and she took a step away.

"I am sure I don't know what you mean."

"Who gave it to you?"

"It was given to me as a gift at Rothbury. It was from a titled man although I can't remember his name." What she said wasn't all a lie, just a twisted version of the truth.

"Are you sure it wasn't from a thief by the name of Jacob? Because if I find you have been meeting with him in secret, there will be hell to pay."

"Who is Jacob?" she asked, trying to keep the quaver from her voice as well as to sound convincing that she had no idea of the man. "I don't know who you mean."

"Sir Jacob Quincey is now nothing more than an outcast and a thief because he murdered a bishop three years ago, as well as tried to steal my wife."

"He did what?" She hadn't known about the wife part.

"That's right." The man straightened his tunic and fixed his weapon belt. "He's a murderer who likes to steal things that don't belong to him. You'd do well to remember that. Now, give me my late wife's dagger." He held out his open palm. When she did nothing to hand it over, he reached for it.

"Nay," she said, pulling her sword from the sheath on her back. It was an involuntary reaction for her to draw her blade whenever she felt threatened. But when she saw the look of anger in the High Sheriff's eyes, she wished she hadn't reacted so quickly.

"You'd better not pull a blade on me unless you intend to use it. So, let's see how good you are with the thing." He chuckled and drew his sword, lunging for her in one swift motion. He took her by surprise. If she hadn't moved to the side quickly, he would have struck her.

"You'd really strike down your own betrothed?" she spat. "What kind of a man are you?"

"What kind of a woman are you that you carry so many weapons and then refuse to use them? Fight me, or I'll have you flayed."

"I cannot believe what I'm hearing."

"Do it," growled the man, lunging at her again.

This time, Maira didn't hesitate. She raised her sword and blocked his blow. The sound of metal clashing against metal echoed through the room. He continued to come after her, backing her into a corner.

"Not bad . . . for a wench!" he commented with a chuckle. Then he came at her fast and furious as if he had gone mad. She did all she could to hold him off, but with her back against the wall and nowhere to go, there wasn't much she could do.

He reached out and flung her to the ground and then covered her body with his. "I will break your spirit, wench, one way or another." He forced his dry, cracked lips upon hers as he kissed her. She closed her eyes and turned her head, unable to move because he had her pinned down. She was a small woman and without her weapons she was no match for any man.

Not wanting to succumb to the evil man, she did whatever she could to stop him. She bit his lip, drawing blood. The iron tang assaulted her tongue. He screamed out and sat up. When he did, she brought her knee up to meet with his groin. When he doubled over in pain, she shot to her feet, grabbing her sword once again.

"My lord," came a man's voice from outside the door.

"What is it?" the High Sheriff yelled, holding one hand to his groin and the other to his lip.

"The men are in the practice yard waiting for you so they can begin."

"This is far from over," snapped Sir Gregory through gritted teeth, getting to his feet. He reached out and snatched the jeweled dagger from her. Rather than fight him again, she let him have it. "Now, take off your sword and daggers and put them on the bed. I will send one of my guards to collect them."

"I won't," she objected.

"You will do it, if I have to take them by force."

When he reached out for her, she backed away. She didn't want him touching her again. "All right, I'll do it," she snapped, unclasping the buckle of the halter, removing her sword first. "But when my father hears about this, you'll be the one with hell to pay. He won't let you treat me this way." She tossed the sword onto the bed and then did the same with her daggers.

The man seemed to think about this for a moment. No one wanted one, or possibly all three bastards of the crown coming after him. Her words must have concerned him because he changed his decision.

"I will let you keep the weapons but you cannot remove them from this room. If I find that to be true, I will take them from you no matter what your father says. You have one last chance to correct your behavior. Do you understand? No wife of mine will be wielding blades."

Maira nodded, biting her tongue hard to keep quiet, trying to restrain herself from saying what she really wanted to say.

If she spoke now, she would most likely offend him again and then her weapons would be confiscated for good.

"Meet me later in the great hall for the meal, Wife."

"I'm not your wife," she said under her breath.

"We're going to remedy that sooner than you think."

"What do you mean?" she asked, feeling the thumping of her rapidly beating heart all the way up to her throat.

"What I mean is that in three days' time, I will have the Bishop of Durham here to help celebrate St. Catherine's Day. I am leaving in the morning for a few days to collect him and escort him back to the castle. But as soon as we return, he will perform the ceremony that will make you my wife."

"Nay, you can't do that," she protested. "I was granted permission from the late King Edward to choose which man I marry. I cannot be forced."

"On the contrary, I have sent a request to King Richard to revoke that privilege since Edward is dead."

"Richard is my cousin. He won't agree to that."

"Are you so sure? Because I believe that he will."

* * *

"SIR JACOB, you can't keep sneaking inside the castle or you're going to get caught." Will followed behind Jacob as they stopped their horses at the edge of the woods just before reaching Durham Castle.

"I have to," said Jacob, dismounting and wrapping a dark cloak around him. "I think I made a mistake by telling Lady Maira my plan. I did it impulsively without thinking it through. I have to make sure she doesn't reveal my secret to the High Sheriff, or all my hard work will be for naught."

"Do you really think she'd tell?"

"I don't know. I thought I could convince her to side with me, but now I'm not so sure."

"Just let it go," Will urged him. "It is taking away from our training back at camp. The festival is in a few days and the villagers need more help to prepare for the attack."

"Nay." Jacob shook his head, looking at the ground. "I can't concentrate, because all I can think about is Lady Maira."

"You are infatuated with the girl, and that's not good." Will shook his head and made a tsking sound with his mouth. "She is going to be your undoing, my lord."

"Nay, I don't think so." Jacob hoped Will wasn't right. "If I can just talk to her once more, I am sure I can get her to see things my way."

"And if she doesn't?" asked Will. "Then what will you do?"

Jacob ran a weary hand through his hair, narrowing his eyes and surveying the castle. "I don't want to think about that. All I know is that I have strong feelings for Maira, though I barely know her. I can't and I won't let her marry the High Sheriff. He took Catherine from me and I'll not let him take Maira as well."

"I think this is more about a vendetta against the High Sheriff than anything else."

"Not true."

"You don't need to worry," Will told him. "I hear the daughters of the bastard triplets have been granted permission to agree to whom they marry."

"Then I'll convince her to marry me instead." Jacob felt possessed by this woman and he couldn't let it go.

"Marry you? Why would she marry you?"

"Because I am going to be not only the lord of the castle, but High Sheriff, too. She'll want me. I'll make sure she does."

"If she only wanted a man who was lord of the castle and High Sheriff then she would marry Sir Gregory, wouldn't she?"

God, Jacob hoped not. He needed to talk to Maira and explain to her everything that happened because he didn't think she really believed him. The last thing he wanted was for her to think he killed a bishop, which is something he would never do.

"I'm going to tell her everything, Will."

"Everything?" asked Will in surprise. "Are you sure that's a wise idea? It might do the opposite and frighten her away."

"I want her to know everything about me before she makes her choice of whom to marry. I don't want to keep secrets from the woman I want to be my wife."

* * *

MAIRA SAT at the dais next to Sir Gregory later that day for the meal, watching the High Sheriff make a fool of himself.

"More wine," he said, raising his goblet. He shared a trencher and cup with Maira as was custom. But after seeing how he ate like a pig, she didn't want to touch anything on her plate let alone the goblet. "Bring more venison and squirrel stew," ordered the man, waving a hand in the air. He clamped his greasy fingers over the goblet taking a big swallow of wine. Then he handed the cup to her.

"Nay, but thank you," she said, flashing a smile. "I'm not feeling well and don't think I'll eat or drink anything. If you don't mind I'd like to go back to my chamber and lie down."

"Go!" the man snorted. "But don't even think of leaving the castle because I've put extra men on patrol to make certain you don't try to sneak out again."

"Of course not," she said, pushing up from her chair. When she did, she heard little Ricker crying from across the great hall.

"Shut him up," called out Sir Gregory. "I tire of hearing the boy cry all the time. Take him to the bedchamber and keep him there for the rest of the night."

That angered Maira. She turned back to the man. "If you'd treat your son a little kinder then mayhap he wouldn't be so frightened of you that he has to cry."

"He's not frightened of me. And I'm his father and will treat him however I want."

"Well, I don't like it." She put her hands on her hips.

"Really." He looked at her over the edge of the goblet and slowly put the cup down. "And how do you suggest I treat the boy?"

"A good father would protect his son. He would take him on outings and spend time getting to know him instead of constantly pushing him away. Instead of punishing the lad, you could try . . . playing with him. Aye," she said with a nod of her head. "I'm sure little Ricker would like that."

"I see." He perused her, chewing his food and licking his lips. "Then that is what we'll do."

"Good," she said, feeling as if she'd done something to help the boy.

"While I'm away, you will take the nursemaid's place and tend to the boy yourself."

"Me?" Maira asked in surprise. "But I thought –"

"Starting tomorrow morning, Ricker will be at your side every minute of the day."

"Why me?" she asked.

"Because you will soon be his mother, just like you said. So you will play with him, go on outings, and do whatever it takes to make him happy and stop his bloody crying."

"But that's not what I meant." Maira didn't want to take care of a toddler. She needed to plan her escape and a way to get out of marrying the cur. She didn't want to be saddled with taking care of his offspring as well.

"You'll do it. Now, go to bed since you aren't feeling well. In the morning, the nursemaid will bring the boy to you and you'll take care of him until my return."

"Aye, my lord," she said softly, making her way down the dais. Once again, her mouth had gotten her into a situation where she didn't want to be involved.

Maira made her way quickly out of the great hall, heading toward her solar. As she passed by the corridor with the tapestry hiding the secret entrance to the tunnel, she swore from the corner of her eye she saw the wall tapestry move.

"Tommy?" she whispered, looking over her shoulder and then down the dark corridor. She wanted to make certain the boy was all right after what he went through the other day. She also wanted to apologize since she promised him a pair of shoes and he still didn't have any.

Going back to her chamber was probably the wise thing to do, but her curiosity and longing to see the little boy and his mother again made her head down the darkened corridor instead of up the stairs to her bedchamber.

Looking over her shoulder once more, she pushed aside

the wall hanging and slipped through the small opening into the tunnel.

"I wish I would have brought a candle," she mumbled to herself, heading down the dark passageway made of stone. The floor beneath her feet was nothing but earth. Using her hand on the wall as a guide, she slowly continued forward. Before long, she heard a noise behind her and stopped. "Tommy? Is that you?" When she had no answer, her heart picked up in pace. "Who's there?" she called out a bit louder, wishing for her weapons at a time like this.

She turned around to head back out the entrance and when she did she crashed into someone. As she opened her mouth to scream, a large hand covered her mouth.

"Don't make another peep," mumbled a deep voice in her ear.

CHAPTER 11

"*D*on't scream Maira, or you're going to give away our secret."

Maira recognized the voice of Jacob and calmed immediately. Once he removed his hand from her mouth, she turned to try to see him in the dark.

"What are you doing here, Jacob?" she whispered.

"I'm here to see you." Without seeing it coming, she felt his lips on hers. It felt good and she welcomed the kiss. Then his arms went around her, pulling her closer as he hugged her to his chest. "I don't want to lose you to him," he said.

"Him? Who are you talking about?" she mumbled into his chest. "And stop holding me so tightly. I can barely breathe."

"The High Sheriff," said Jacob, loosening his grip. "I won't let him take you the way he did Catherine."

"Catherine," she repeated, feeling suddenly less excited. She wasn't exactly sure what Jacob meant, but felt a tinge of jealousy when he said the woman's name.

"Even though I didn't know this woman, I won't be a

replacement for her in your game of vengeance against Sir Gregory."

"It's more than that, Maira. You see, I want you to be mine."

"Yours?" she exclaimed, her head spinning right now.

"Shhhh," he said, putting his finger against her lips. "I want to talk to you but not here. These tunnels lead to every room in the castle. If we can hear what is going on inside the chambers, they might be able to hear us in here as well."

"So how is it that you know about the tunnels and so do the servants, but not the High Sheriff?"

"When he stole the castle at the death of Lord Emery, he didn't know and I instructed the servants to keep the tunnels a secret."

"Lord Emery?" she asked. "The last lord of the castle?"

"Aye. Lady Catherine's father. We'll talk in your chamber," said Jacob, taking her by the hand and leading her through the dark passageways.

"Slow down," she said, almost stumbling in the dark. Jacob stopped and removed something from the wall. When he did, light streamed in from somewhere. "What is that?" she whispered. She saw his eye light up as he peered into the hole.

"Look," he said, putting his hands around her waist and holding her in front of the peephole. She stood on her toes and was able to see into the room. She almost gasped aloud when she saw Sir Gregory enter the room, holding the hand of a maidservant.

"Take off your clothes," ordered Sir Gregory.

"Aye, my lord." The young woman started to lift her gown but before she could remove her clothes the High Sheriff had dropped his breeches and was bending her over the bed.

"I can't watch," said Maira, making a face, pulling away from the peephole. A shiver of disgust ran through her body.

"That's the man you're going to marry," said Jacob, plugging up the hole in the wall.

"Nay! I'll never marry him," she remarked.

"Come," he told her leading her further. She heard him fumbling with something and then heard a scraping sound. Firelight lit up his face. He held a tallow candle in one hand.

"Where did you get that?" she asked in surprise.

"It was here all along, you just have to know where to find it. This way," he said, leading her to a hidden staircase.

"Where does this lead?" she asked, staring up the narrow stone staircase in awe.

"It leads to the second floor. Are you staying in the room in the far east wing?"

"I am. Why?" she asked him.

"Good," was all he said. Still holding his hand, they climbed the stairs and then he led her down another corridor. As they passed one chamber after another, she got glimpses of people and heard snippets of conversations from through the peepholes in the rooms.

"Why are there so many peepholes?" she asked.

"It is a way for the lord of the castle to spy on his guests that sometimes turn out to be enemies."

"It seems so invading."

"They don't know about it, so it's not a problem. There are other reasons for the peepholes, too."

"Like what?"

He stopped in his tracks and turned toward her. The flame of the candle lit up his handsome face in a soft glow. "It is a way for the consummations of marriages to be witnessed without making the bride feel uncomfortable with half a dozen men and a priest watching from the foot of the bed. Witnesses are required for every wedding night. Lord Emery thought when his daughter married, this would be an easier way for her to accept the custom."

"Oh," she said, holding her hand to her mouth. Why is it she had never known about this? "So, did you witness the wedding night of Lady Catherine and Sir Gregory through a hole in the wall?"

"Nay. I made sure the hole to her chamber was covered and that no one could find it."

"You didn't want anyone seeing her naked?"

"That, and I didn't want anyone seeing me coupling with her either."

Maira's eyes opened wide. "She was your lover!"

"Aye."

"Then Sir Gregory was telling the truth when he said you tried to steal his wife. How appalling of you to do such a thing."

"Nay, you don't understand, Maira. It's not like that at all." He pushed on the wall and a spring-loaded door opened into what she realized was her bedchamber.

"I can't believe it. My chamber has a secret door." Impressed, Maira inspected the opening.

"This will make it easier for you to slip away to visit me in the woods."

He walked inside the room and she followed. Then he closed the secret door that was right next to the hearth. Putting the candle down on the table, he turned back to her once again. "I want to tell you everything about me, Maira. I want you to know things before you make your decision of who you want to marry."

"I'm not marrying anyone," she said, walking past him to the bed. She picked up one of her daggers and shined it on her sleeve.

JACOB FELT nervous about revealing all his secrets to Maira. But if he didn't, she would think he was naught but a scoundrel. "Sit down, Maira. I want to finish telling you about Lady Catherine."

"I'm not sure I want to know." She continued to look down at her blade.

He walked up behind her and placed his hands on her shoulders. Then he bent over and whispered in her ear. "I really want you to know everything about me."

Noticing her eyes close slightly, and the way she turned her head exposing her neck to him, he realized she had feelings for him as well. He wanted nothing more than to kiss her neck and taste her sweet scent upon his tongue.

"Go ahead," she said, giving him the permission he needed. He nibbled at her neck, his tongue gently touching her skin.

"Stop it." She pulled out of his arms and turned around. Her dagger was gripped tightly in her hand.

"You just told me to go ahead. I thought you wanted me to kiss you."

"I meant go ahead with your story. Nothing else."

Jacob walked over to the other side of the room, plopping down on a chair. "Where do I start?" He leaned forward and put his face in his hands.

"Tell me about Lady Catherine." Maira sat down on the bed.

"I thought you didn't want to hear about her."

"I've changed my mind. Why did you try to steal another man's wife?"

"Nay." His head popped up. "You've got it all wrong. Lord Emery favored me. I was his Captain of the Guard. He gave his daughter's hand to me in marriage, but he passed away before we could say our vows. His funeral took the place of the wedding. Lady Catherine was distraught. Her mother had died years before and she had no siblings. Her father was everything to her."

"I see."

"I was to inherit the castle at his death. That is, since I would be his daughter's husband."

"But you weren't."

"Nay, not yet. I was also to become the High Sheriff of Durham. But then Sir Gregory arrived with a bishop from Somerset as well as the pope."

"The pope?" she asked, sounding confused. "Whatever for?"

"That's what I wanted to know. They were supposedly here because of the death of Lord Emery. But the next morning, Sir Gregory sent me to the bishop's room to fetch him for the main meal. I found the man hanging by his neck from a rope attached to the rafters. He had been murdered."

"Murdered? How awful. And you were blamed for it?"

"I immediately used my dagger and cut the man down. Sir Gregory and the pope entered just as the bishop fell into my arms. Of course, it didn't look good for me."

"I suppose not."

"Sir Gregory was able to convince the pope to have my title stripped and to excommunicate me from the church."

"But didn't you get a fair trial?"

"Nay. It seems our weasel, Sir Gregory, had already convinced the king to give him the title of High Sheriff instead of me."

"I can't believe my cousin did that."

He felt jolted for a moment until he remembered that King Richard was Maira's cousin. "To make matters worse, Lady Catherine had returned the jeweled dagger to me that morning. It was my betrothal present to her. A stone was loose and I was going to fix it for her. Lady Catherine loved that dagger and everyone knew it. She took it with her everywhere. Sir Gregory knew about it, since he would visit Lord Emery often. Well, without thinking, I used it to cut down the dead bishop."

"And why should that matter?"

"Because when Sir Gregory saw the dagger in my hand, it made it obvious I had been with her the night before."

"And had you?" Maira crossed her arms over her chest.

"Of course I had. She needed comforting. Her father had just died. Besides, I was her betrothed. But Sir Gregory spun more webs of deceit, convincing the pope that before Lord Emery died, he promised Lady Catherine as well as the castle to him."

"I am so sorry."

"Not as sorry as I was. You see, I bedded Catherine right before that happened. So when Sir Gregory married her and found out she wasn't a virgin, he beat her."

"How awful!"

"I was banned from the castle and sent away with nothing

but my squire at my side. And Will came with me of his own accord."

"Then Sir Gregory truly did steal everything from you."

"Aye, he did." Jacob got up and walked slowly over to Maira. "But he will not have you, Maira. I won't let that cur treat you badly. Please, don't marry him."

"Don't worry, I have no intention of marrying Sir Gregory."

"I am nothing like the High Sheriff nor will I ever be," he said, hoping she would see him for the man he used to be, not the man he was now.

"Of course you're not. I believe you," she said, seeming as if she needed a little convincing. He pulled her into his arms, kissing her once again.

"Jacob, when you kiss me I feel weak in the knees," she whispered.

"I feel the same way," he told her, taking her face in his hands and kissing her deeply, not able to pull away. He only meant to make her heady, but before he knew what happened, he was laying her back on the bed and his hand was sneaking up under her gown.

MAIRA SHOULD HAVE STOPPED JACOB, but she couldn't. Something inside her sprang to life at his touch and made her want him desperately. His story made her feel sorry for him, and she found herself wanting to make him feel happy again.

He continued to kiss her as he leaned over her atop the bed. His hand skimmed up her leg and under her gown, traveling slowly closer and closer to her womanhood. The action was seductive and made her feel aroused. A heat encompassed her and a pulsing sensation started up between her thighs.

"Come with me, Maira. We will go back to the woods and far away from here."

"Jacob, you don't know what you're asking." She felt his other hand skim up her side and cup her breast. Then he kissed her with even more passion and his thumb skimmed over her nipple, bringing it to a peak. She arched up off the bed, never having felt this way before. "Take me," she whispered, feeling as if she didn't know who she was anymore. She was so aroused that she was almost ready to reach her peak. It didn't take much from a man like Jacob before she was dropping her inhibitions and throwing care to the wind. Thoughts, crazy thoughts, filled her head of making love to him right there, right now. The idea scared her and excited her both at the same time.

He suddenly sat up and ran a hand through his hair.

"What's the matter?" she asked him. "Why are you stopping?"

"Nay. This isn't right." He scooted off the bed leaving her lying there in heated passion, ready to fall over the brink. "I won't do this," he mumbled, straightening his tunic and heading back for the secret door.

"Wait!" Maira shot off the bed, feeling so wanton. Her actions embarrassed her now. She felt as if she'd made a mistake.

"You know where to find me if you're interested in joining me on my mission."

"That's it?" she cried, ready to slug him for teasing her and leaving her hanging. "How can you say you want to marry me and almost couple with me one minute and the next be cold and unemotional, walking out the door?"

"I made a mistake in the past and I will not make it again."

"So is that what I am now? A mistake? If that's how you feel, then go. Leave! I don't need you. I don't need anyone but myself." She held back the tears not wanting him to see how upset she was by this. She needed to remain strong.

"Maira, you don't understand." He took two steps toward her and reached out to cup her cheek, but she didn't let him. She turned her head and held up a halting hand.

"Go, before I call the guards and tell them you are here."

"I still want you, Maira, but not like this. I need to take care of unfinished business first."

"I'll not be part of your deceitful, vengeful scheme, so do not ask me again."

"How can you say that after everything I've told you? Don't stay with the bastard, Maira. Please."

"Don't call Sir Gregory a bastard. After all, have you forgotten, my father and uncles are bastards?"

"I didn't mean it like that." His gray eyes bored into her, holding desperation as well as remorse and confusion. "I just want things to be different, that's all."

There came a knock at the door and the voice of a woman from the other side. "Lady Maira, may I come in?"

"Go," she whispered to Jacob.

"I don't want to leave you this way." He looked at the door and then back to the secret passageway.

"If you don't leave right now, I'll tell the woman to enter and then your secret will no longer be a secret."

"All right, I'll leave," he said, seeming very hesitant to go now. "But promise me one thing. Promise me you'll give me one more chance before you make a decision about me. Come to my hidden camp in the woods tomorrow and let me make it up to you."

"I'll promise nothing of the sort. Now go."

He nodded slowly and headed out the secret passageway, closing the door behind him.

Maira's heart about broke, but she had to let Jacob go. After what almost happened between them, she might have made the biggest mistake of her life.

"Enter," she called out. The door to the room opened and Cleo poked her head inside the room.

"Cleo? What are you doing here?" Maira rushed over to greet her.

"I brought you some food, my lady." Cleo held a basket over her arm. "Tommy told me you left the great hall before you'd had a chance to eat."

"It's dangerous for you to be roaming the corridor. What if Sir Gregory sees you? You'll be punished."

"The High Sheriff is well in his cups and has already retired to his solar for the evening."

"Oh, that's right," said Maira, remembering she saw the man with a servant girl in his room through the peephole. "Come inside, quickly and close the door."

"Nay, I am not allowed in the chamber of a noble." Cleo shook her head.

"Please. Just for a minute. You can use the secret passageway leading from this room to get back to the kitchen. The High Sheriff will never know you were here."

"Did Sir Jacob leave yet?" Cleo stepped inside and scanned the room.

"You knew he was here?"

"Aye. Tommy and Alf told me. They saw him in the tunnels."

"Cleo, can I ask you a few questions?"

"Of course, my lady."

"Have a seat." Maira pointed to a chair. Once Cleo sat, Maira placed the basket on the table and pulled out a hunk of bread. She broke off a piece and handed it to Cleo.

"That is white bread, my lady. I am a servant and eat brown bread only," the woman told her.

"Tonight you'll eat what I eat because you are my guest." She handed the bread to Cleo and pulled out a goblet and filled it with wine from a decanter. Offering it to Cleo, she nodded.

"I couldn't."

"I insist."

"Thank you, my lady."

Maira sat on the chair across from the woman and they shared a meal together as they talked.

"I am wondering about Lady Catherine," Maira told her.

"What about her?"

"So she was Jacob's lover?" It almost embarrassed her to ask since a moment ago she had almost been the man's lover.

"It's not for me to say, my lady."

"You must know. Please tell me."

"Aye, they were lovers and would have been married if Sir Gregory hadn't come to Durham Castle."

"So Jacob was telling the truth."

"When the bishop was discovered dead, Sir Jacob was blamed for it."

"Do you think he did it?" asked Maira, digging into the basket and pulling out a sweetmeat next.

"Nay, of course not. Sir Jacob would never do such a thing and everyone knows it."

"Everyone but the pope," said Maira, picking up the goblet and taking a sip of wine.

"The pope and Sir Gregory have always been close. Or at least that's what I hear." Cleo peeked into the basket and used two fingers to snag a piece of cheese. She held it in the air as she continued talking. "Before any of us knew what happened, Sir Gregory had convinced the pope to excommunicate Sir Jacob. Jacob lost everything, even his title."

"So I hear." Maira didn't like that Sir Gregory had deceived people in high positions. She thought of bringing this to the attention of her cousin, King Richard, but the pope ranked higher than the king when it came to situations such as excommunicating a knight. Nay. She had to find a way to tell the pope the truth.

"What about that jeweled dagger? The one that was once Lady Catherine's?" asked Maira.

"Oh, that dagger wasn't hers. Not at first."

"Sir Jacob said he gave it to her."

"Aye. It once belonged to Sir Jacob's late mother. He treasured the blade more than anything. We all knew he really loved Lady Catherine when he gave it to her at their betrothal."

"So they were really almost married?"

"Aye and nay." Cleo ate the cheese and followed it down with more wine before she continued. "They were betrothed by word of mouth, but the announcements were never posted. Before that could happen, Lord Emery died, and Sir Gregory swooped in and took over."

"Just like that?" said Maira.

"Sir Gregory is a man known for getting exactly what he wants."

"Well, he's not going to get everything he wants." Maira threw the bread down on the table and stood up in a huff.

"What do you mean, my lady?"

"I'm not going to marry him and that's all there is to it."

"Can you do that? I thought you were betrothed?"

"I was, but as soon as my father finds out what this man is like, he will break the betrothal."

"Then you need to get a message to your father quickly."

"Morag and Branton left here and are going to tell him. They'll stop in Rothbury where they'll send a missive to him in Whitehaven."

"Whitehaven? A messenger will never be able to get there and back before your wedding. The High Sheriff has told us to prepare the wedding feast and that in three days' time you will be married to him."

Maira walked over and picked up her crown from the dressing table. She ran a finger over the gemstones, thinking about the promise she'd been given as a child. "The late king told me that it was our grandmother's wish – Queen Philippa that my cousins and I would be able to agree whom we marry. But it looks as if the High Sheriff is going to change that as well."

"Was that the queen's crown?" asked Cleo.

"Aye, it was. She left each of us a crown and this heart brooch." Maira moved her hair aside and showed Cleo the brooch. Cleo's mouth fell open and her hand stilled. The bread dropped to the table.

"That brooch. I know it well," said Cleo in a soft voice.

"How could you?" asked Maira. "There are only a few of

them and each of them has been a present from the late queen."

Cleo stood up and put her hand in her pocket. She held it out and opened it. Maira's eyes focused upon a heart brooch resting in her palm.

"You, Cleo? You have one, too?"

"I was once a chosen one as well," said the woman in a near whisper.

"Chosen for what?" Maira tested her, waiting for the answer before she continued to speak.

"I'm a Follower of the Secret Heart just like you, Lady Maira."

It shocked Maira to hear the woman say the right words. At first she thought mayhap Cleo had found the brooch or stolen it but by the tears in the woman's eyes, she knew her story was true.

"I don't understand," said Maira. "How could you have been chosen? You're just a commoner."

"Less than that, I'm a servant," said Cleo. "The good queen gave me the brooch right after I stopped her from eating tainted meat one day. I used to cook for the king and queen many years ago."

"You did?"

"Aye. I knew something was wrong, and I tasted the meat myself before I served it. I became deathly ill, but was able to stop the meal from being served. When the queen found out that I risked my life to save hers, she not only paid dearly for the best physicians to heal me, but she made me a member of her secret group. She said I was a strong woman and someday would do honorable and memorable things."

"And did you?" asked Maira excitedly. "Did you stop a war like Fia, or stop a thief like my cousin, Willow?"

"Nay. I did nothing," said the woman sadly, stroking the brooch in her hand. "I became pregnant with the kennel-groom's baby. When Harold died on a hunt by accident, I could no longer bear to stay. I left and came here to work as a cook." Tears fell from her eyes. "I don't deserve this brooch, Maira. After Harold died, I would have killed myself if I hadn't been pregnant with Tommy. I had no will to live. Take the brooch. I don't deserve it."

"Nay. You put that brooch back, but not in your pocket. You wear it proudly on your chest instead."

"I'm afraid to do that," said Cleo. "If the High Sheriff sees it, he'll accuse me of stealing it and he'll punish me. Or he'll take it for himself."

"You're right," said Maira, putting her hand around the woman's shoulders. "But don't worry, because soon Sir Gregory will be gone and Sir Jacob will be lord of the castle like he should have been in the first place."

"What are you saying, my lady? Sir Jacob is an outcast and has also been excommunicated from the church. He has no title or lands at all."

"He is also going to change all that and I am going to help him do it."

"What do you mean? What can you do that could bring about such a difference?"

"I will tell you all about it, but not yet," said Maira. "But when the time comes, I may need to count on you to be strong and to help us."

"I would do anything to see Sir Jacob back in the castle and Sir Gregory gone."

"Then tell the other servants to stand by because this might take help from all of you to make it happen."

"Are you going to lead some kind of revolt against Sir Gregory, my lady?"

"Not me, Cleo. But I know someone else who will."

CHAPTER 12

*M*aira rushed back to her chamber right after Sir Gregory left with his small entourage the next morning. Now that he was gone, she had every intention of collecting her weapons and heading to the woods to meet with Jacob. He would be glad to know she had decided to join him in his battle after all.

The High Sheriff was a horrible man. The way he treated people was even worse. He overtaxed the villagers and demanded them to give him even their share of food. He didn't see to the needs of his servants and only thought about himself. And the way he treated his own son was not acceptable at all.

If Maira's father didn't arrive in time, she was going to have to do something to stop the High Sheriff from trying to marry her. She had told him she had the right to choose her husband, but his comment made her worried. If he was able to convince a pope to excommunicate Jacob, then who knew what else he was capable of doing.

She strapped on her weapons and was about to sneak out using the tunnels when there came a knock at her door.

"Who is it?" she called out, not knowing who would be coming here this early in the morning.

"My lady, it is Teresa," came a woman's muffled voice from the other side of the door.

"Who?" she shouted back, securing her daggers in her waist belt. Before the woman could answer, she heard the crying of a child.

"Ricker," she said in a half-whisper, almost forgetting that the High Sheriff said she was supposed to watch his son in his absence. She rushed over and opened the door. She would have to talk the nursemaid into watching the child, at least until she had time to get to the woods and back.

"Here is the boy and his things." Teresa handed the toddler to Maira. Her hands automatically went out in an act of defense. Instead of keeping the child away, the little boy reached out and clung to her, wrapping his arms around her neck. Then the woman proceeded to hand Maira a travel bag filled with the boy's things.

"Teresa, I'm sorry but I can't watch Ricker right now." She tried to hand the boy back, but he clung to her even tighter.

"Why not?" asked Teresa, sounding very upset.

"I have things to do. Mayhap later."

"But, my lady, the High Sheriff gave me permission to take a trip home to see my family."

"Your family?"

"Aye. My husband and my four children."

"Where are they?" she asked.

"My home is just outside of Scarborough."

"Scarborough?" asked Maira. "But that will take you days just to get there and back."

"I have a wagon waiting for me. The peddler from my hometown was passing through and said he will give me a ride so I won't have to walk. But I have to leave at once."

"Nay. I can't watch the boy. You'll have to do it."

Ricker started wailing in her ear.

"But my lady! My five-month-old daughter is very sick and my husband sent a missive saying he doesn't know if she will even live."

"Sick? Five months old?" This information shocked Maira and her heart went out to the woman. Ricker continued to bawl very loudly.

"Please, let me see my child one last time." The woman looked so forlorn that there was no way Maira could deny her what she needed.

"Teresa, you will go to your family and stay there until your daughter is healed. I will command one of the guards to take you on the back of his horse so it will be faster. He will also protect you on your trip. I want to do anything I can to help you and your family."

"Would you really do that for me, my lady?"

"Not only that, but I'll send our healer on one of the castle's fastest horses to ride with you. If your child is sick then she'll need someone skilled to help her. And take this to feed your family." She untied the coin pouch from her belt and handed it to the woman.

"Thank you, my lady," cried the woman, falling to her knees and putting her head down on Maira's feet.

"Teresa, get up. There is no need for that. Now, go pack your things and I will summon the guard. Now off you go."

Teresa got to her feet, wiping the tears from her eyes. "You won't get in trouble with the High Sheriff for this, will you?" she asked.

"Don't worry about him. I'll take care of everything. Now hurry. You have a sick child waiting."

"Aye, my lady. And thank you ever so much."

Maira looked at the little boy in her arms who was wiping his eyes with his fist.

"Well, Ricker. I think we'll go to the woods for our first outing."

* * *

JACOB FOUND it hard to concentrate on preparing the villagers for the attack. Every time he heard a squirrel scamper through the underbrush, he spun around hoping it was Maira. It was already late afternoon and still she hadn't showed. That concerned him greatly.

"My lord?" Will waved his hand in front of Jacob's face. "Did you want me to train the men myself, or were you planning on jumping in and helping out at all?"

"Oh, I'm sorry, Will." Jacob turned to see a dozen men all staring at him, waiting for his direction in their training. "I've just been a little distracted, that's all. Everyone take a five-minute break and then we'll resume the training."

"A break?" complained Roger. "We're here to learn to fight, not to rest."

"That's right," agreed Gerald. "Some of the men still feel uncomfortable with real weapons in their hands."

"That's true," said Will. "Most of their training through the years has been with the makeshift weapons."

"Then, I suggest we get back to training right away, since there is no time to lose," said a female voice from behind Jacob.

He spun around to find Maira riding through the woods atop her horse.

"Maira, you came!" he exclaimed. But as she rode closer, he realized she wasn't alone. Held protectively in front of her in the saddle was a toddler. "What the hell! Please don't tell me you brought a child here?"

"I did," she said, stopping her horse and dismounting. She lifted the child off the horse and held him in her arms. "This is Ricker," she told him.

"Ricker? God's eyes, don't tell me you brought the High Sheriff's son with you? What were you thinking?"

"There's no need to be upset. The High Sheriff is gone for a few days to collect the Bishop of Durham. And Ricker won't say a word because the boy hasn't talked since his mother died."

"Really." Jacob was leery of the situation but decided it was a risk well worth taking. Maira was here, and that meant she was going to be his, and not Sir Gregory's bride after all.

"Really," she told him. "Now, I'm here to help. So shall we get started?"

"We shall," he said, pleased by what he was hearing. "Why don't you put the boy down and I'll introduce you to the others?"

"All right." She put the boy down but he started crying and clinging to her. She picked him up and he stopped crying.

"This isn't going to work," he told her. "I don't feel good about the child being here. His crying is going to alert someone that we're here."

"There was no one else to watch him," she told Jacob. "And I promised Sir Gregory I'd look after the boy while he was gone. However, it seems like he starts crying unless he's held."

"Here, let me try," he said, reaching out for the boy. The child clung to Maira even tighter, not wanting to go to Jacob. "What's the matter with him?" asked Jacob. "I'm not going to hurt the boy."

"Aye, but he doesn't know that," said Maira. Then she leaned over and whispered to him. "The High Sheriff is not very nice to him and often punishes him and sends him to bed with no food just because of his crying."

"No food?" This angered Jacob and made him hate Sir Gregory even more. "Mayhap, the boy is hungry. Will, get me some bread," commanded Jacob.

"Aye, my lord." Will walked over and handed him a loaf of bread.

"Not an entire loaf. He's just a child," scoffed Jacob, breaking off a piece and holding it out to the boy. "Here you are, Son," he said, not sure why he'd used that endearment. It just sort of floated off his tongue before he could stop it.

Ricker peeked out, still holding tightly to Maira, having had his head buried against her chest.

"It's all right," Maira told the toddler. "Jacob is our friend. I promise you that he will never hurt you."

The little boy slowly reached out a trembling hand to take the bread from Jacob. Then he shoved the whole piece in his mouth at once.

"You're not jesting that the little tyke is hungry. Will, I'm going to need the rest of that bread after all."

"Aye, my lord," said Will, handing him the loaf.

Something about seeing Maira holding the boy touched

Jacob's heart. Here was a rebellious woman dressed for battle with daggers at her waist and a sword on her back. He chuckled when she pushed back her hood and he saw that she wore the late queen's jeweled crown.

"What's so funny?" she asked, becoming instantly defensive as was her nature.

"There is nothing as beautiful as a hardened warrior woman wearing a crown and cradling a toddler. It becomes you, Lady Maira. I could see you being a very protective mother."

"Y-you could?"

With her head down, her innocent, bright blue eyes flashed up to him curiously. She was an angel in disguise. Beneath the gruff exterior, he saw right through to the soft, caring side that Maira kept hidden.

"You are beautiful," he whispered, reaching out and brushing back a long lock of hair behind her ear. She wet her lips by pressing them together, the tip of her tongue shooting out slightly, making him want to kiss her again.

Then Ricker made a noise and reached out with both his arms to Jacob.

"He wants more bread," said Jacob, holding up the loaf. But Ricker kept reaching for him.

MAIRA COULD SEE VERY WELL what was happening with the child, even if Jacob couldn't. "I think he wants you to hold him," she told Jacob, passing the child to him before he could object.

"But I can't," said Jacob, cradling the boy in his arms and up against his chest. Little Ricker leaned his head against

Jacob and his eyes flitted closed. "I guess he's tired." Jacob ran a gentle hand over the boy's head. For a moment, Maira thought she saw care and love within his eyes. But then his jaw tightened and he shook his head. "We don't have time for this. We need to practice." He looked up to the sky. "It's going to rain soon. Will, put the boy down for a nap in my tent." He handed the boy to Will, but the child started crying and wailing loudly.

"I don't think he likes me much," grumbled Will, trying to bounce the boy and tap him on the back at the same time.

"Keep him quiet or he's going to alert the guards at the castle that we're here."

"I'll take him," said Maira. But even with her holding him and trying to calm him, Ricker kept crying. "I don't know what's wrong with him. I can't get him to stop crying."

"Shall I ask one of the village women to help out?" asked Will.

"Nay. Give me the boy," said Jacob, taking him back into his hold. Instantly, Ricker stopped crying and laid his head against Jacob's chest, closed his eyes and started to suck his thumb.

"Well, look at that!" exclaimed Will. "You have the magic touch, my lord. You seem to be the only one who can keep the boy from crying."

"I don't know about that," he mumbled. "Will, introduce Lady Maira to the others and get them back to practice." He headed toward the tent.

"And where are you going?" asked Maira, finding humor in the situation.

"I'm putting the boy down for his nap. He is overtired as well as hungry. I don't know how no one but me can see that."

As he disappeared into the tent, Maira smiled. Jacob looked good holding a child. She was sure he would make a wonderful father someday. But would he be married to her? She knew he would ask her again to marry him, but she wasn't sure what to say. Maira had never thought she wanted to ever marry a man. And now she had two men who wanted her as their bride. She only came here to help fight, she told herself. So why in Heaven's name was she suddenly thinking about having babies with Sir Jacob?

CHAPTER 13

"That's good, but not so much stabbing motion," Maira instructed one of the villagers two days later. She had spent the last few days at the camp and had brought Ricker who now seldom cried at all. It was almost like he was happy here with Jacob. "That motion makes you vulnerable by exposing your entire upper torso to your opponent. And don't forget to step away from your opponent's attack. It's the simplest method of defense."

"Aye, I understand," said the man. "Thank you, Lady Maira. That makes it so much clearer."

Maira stopped to catch her breath, loving the way it felt to teach others her skill. The training was coming along nicely with the new weapons. But everyone had been so busy and focused these past two days that Maira hadn't had any private time to talk with Jacob. Between teaching the fighting moves to his small army and stopping every so often to play with Ricker, Jacob seemed to barely notice she was there.

"Nay, don't touch that. It's sharp," she heard Jacob tell the child. He hurried over to the tent where Ricker was about to pick up a dagger. "I made something for you last night," he told the boy. "Will? Where is the present I made for Ricker?"

"I'm not sure, my lord. Was I supposed to keep track of it?" Will called out, dueling with Roger.

"Nay, never mind. I'll find it," Jacob answered with a swish of his hand through the air. Then he disappeared into the tent. Maira took this opportunity to approach Will.

"Will, can you watch Ricker for a few minutes?" she asked him. "I'd like to talk to Jacob privately."

"Of course," said Will, bending down and talking gibberish to the boy.

"Squire, he's two years old, not a baby," came Jacob's voice from inside the tent. "Ah, I found it." He pushed open the flap of the tent just as Maira was about to enter. They stood face to face, their bodies slightly touching. In his hand, he held a carved wooden wolf.

"Lady Maira," he said, his breath caressing her forehead as he spoke. "Was there something you needed?"

"I wondered if we could talk in private for a moment."

"Of course. Just let me give this to Ricker first." He headed over to Will and the boy and hunkered down, holding the carved animal behind his back. "Guess what I've got, Ricker? I think it is something you might like to play with." He held out the wolf and the little boy's eyes shone with excitement as he took the piece from Jacob.

"Doggie," said the boy, hugging the wolf and then giving Jacob a hug as well.

Maira's mouth fell open.

"Aye, I suppose it's like a dog," Jacob told the boy. "That is yours to keep." He stood up and brushed off his hands. Maira stared at him in shock. "What are you looking at?" he asked, glancing down to his groin and then back at her. He flashed her a cocky smile.

"Nay, not that," she said, making a face. "Jacob, Ricker spoke. Didn't you hear him say doggie?"

"Aye, I guess he did." Jacob nodded at the boy. Will was still talking gibberish and making the wolf bark now.

"He hasn't spoken a word since his mother passed away," she reminded him.

Jacob's face turned solemn. His whole demeanor changed. "He looks a lot like his mother," he told her. "It only makes me miss Catherine even more."

"I don't know what Lady Catherine looked like, but I will say Ricker looks nothing at all like the High Sheriff."

"Thank God for small miracles," mumbled Jacob. "I feel badly for any child who has that bastard – er, demon, as a father."

Maira knew the reason he changed his word was because she told him her father and uncles were bastards. She smiled slightly. "Thank you, Jacob, but my father and uncles were also known as the Demon Thief as well."

"I give up," he said with a shrug of his shoulders and holding his palms upward. "Did you want to talk to me?"

"Aye. Can we go inside the tent?"

"I have a better idea. Why don't we take a few minutes and go for a walk? I know a secluded, soft knoll near the river that I'd like to show you." He held out his hand.

"All right. I'd like that." She took his hand and they strolled over to his horse.

"You'll need to leave this here." He reached around her and slid her sword from the holster on her back, setting it atop a rock.

"Nay. I don't go anywhere without my weapons." She reached for it, but his fingers closed around her wrist to stop her.

"Trust me," he told her. "It'll only get in the way." Then to her surprise, he lifted her up atop his horse and followed by mounting behind her.

"Oh, we're going to ride there." She still didn't feel comfortable about leaving her sword. She looked over her shoulder for it but when she did, she saw his smiling face up close.

"Don't worry. Will is there and will look out for it."

"But what about Ricker? I shouldn't leave him."

"The boy is busy playing with his new toy. Besides, he is safe with Will."

"You put a lot of trust in Will, don't you?"

"A knight trusts his squire with his life."

"And you trust Will?" She turned forward, feeling the slight stubble of his cheek against hers when he leaned closer, pressing up against her to grab the reins.

"Aye," he answered, so close to her that it sent a shudder of delight right through her. The scent of pine and a freshness like morning dew drifted from his body, filling her senses. In Jacob's arms, she felt safe and secure. And it oddly felt right, instead of wrong. She never thought she needed a man, but his presence in her life right now seemed to fill a dark void with light.

"You are very good with children," she said to make conversation as they rode.

"I have a brother who is quite a bit younger than me," he told her. "He idolized me and I looked after him all the time since my mother was often ill."

"What was the matter with your mother?" asked Maira.

"She always became deathly sick whenever she was pregnant."

"How often was that?"

"She was pregnant four times. My sister died when she was only two. My mother died birthing another daughter. The baby didn't make it either."

"I am so sorry," she told him as they got to a creek and he slid off the horse.

"It's part of life, and I had no choice but to accept it," said Jacob, holding out his arms for her to dismount. "It's never easy to get used to death. My father died in battle before I was old enough to fight alongside him. What about your family, Maira?"

"Well, you know about my father, and my mother is a noblewoman named Cordelia. She was a widow when she married my father and thought she couldn't have children. But that proved to be wrong. I am the eldest and I have four brothers, William, Philip, Theodore and my ten-year-old brother, Michael."

"It must be nice to have so many siblings."

"What about your brother? What happened to him?" Maira let him guide her to the ground.

"Frank decided to join the church. His life turned to prayer. He's a priest now in Hartlepool. So, you see, I am the last chance to carry on the family name since my brother is worthless."

"Worthless? Is that really how you see him?" It surprised her that he would say such a thing.

"It is."

"Do you ever talk with your brother?"

"Nay. I became angry with him when he left to join the priesthood. I wanted him to learn to fight and be a knight like me. We haven't spoken in years."

"Fighting isn't right for everyone, Jacob. Mayhap, you need to let your bygones go."

"I admire anyone who can handle a blade. You are a woman and yet you can fight like a man. My brother is weak and could never protect himself or anyone else. He'll never amount to anything. My father wanted both of us to be warriors, and he'd stir in his grave to know that Frank let him down."

"He's a priest!" she reminded him. "How is that letting anyone down? He is doing the work of God. Besides, you're no longer a knight. The way I see it, you're naught but a thief. So, mayhap, you let your father down as well."

"Don't say that. It's not the truth. I told you I was framed." His jaw ticked in aggravation.

"I'm sorry, Jacob. I didn't mean that. Shall we visit the knoll now?"

JACOB GUIDED Maira to the knoll of soft grass, feeling shaken by their conversation. He had wanted to bring her here to possibly spend a little intimate time with her. But now, disturbing thoughts filled his head, ruining the moment.

Maira sounded as if she thought he were worthless, when it was the furthest thing from the truth. Or was it? Perhaps she was right in saying he let his father down. His father wouldn't have waited three years to make matters right. Nay, he would have turned right around and had his revenge with the High Sheriff on the spot if this situation had happened to him. This whole thing made Jacob feel ill. But Maira's next question made him feel even worse.

"So, were you in love with Lady Catherine?" Maira bent down and picked a daisy as they walked.

"What?" He stalled since he didn't know how to reply.

"It couldn't have been easy to lose her to the High Sheriff."

"Nay, it wasn't." Jacob's throat went dry and he shook his head. It was an extremely warm day for being so late in the year.

The sun shone down on Maira's strawberry-blond hair, making it glow like an angel. She wore that crown wherever she went, and the gemstones winked in the light, taunting him, making him remember all that he once almost had and then lost.

"I heard from the cook that the jeweled dagger was once your mother's and you gave it to Catherine."

"I did." His eyes went to her waist belt but the jeweled dagger was no longer there. "Where is my dagger, Maira?"

She sniffed the daisy and looked up at him with wide, blue eyes. Then she twirled the flower between her fingers as she spoke.

"I don't have it. The High Sheriff stole it from me right after our sword fight."

"You fought with him, Maira?" asked Jacob with concern.

"He ordered me to, right after he told me that I wasn't allowed to wear my weapons anymore."

"Then why do you still have them?"

"I used the name of my father and uncles to force him to let me keep them. After all, no one wants the wrath of the Legendary Bastard Triplets on their head."

"Nay, I suppose not. Your father and uncles are legends and also still feared by most in the land."

"Sometimes, that works in my favor," she said with a smile that lit up her whole face.

"Sir Gregory didn't hurt you, did he?" asked Jacob, feeling his blood boil at the thought of the man.

"He didn't, but he almost forced himself on me. Thank goodness a page came to the door and interrupted."

"He – he almost . . . raped you?" asked Jacob, barely able to even say the words.

Maira's smile turned to a frown and she threw the daisy to the ground. "It doesn't matter because it won't happen again." She turned to walk away but he reached out and took her by the shoulders to stop her.

"It does matter, Maira. No man will treat you that way and get away with it. I'll make sure of it."

She glanced back over her shoulder at him and then her gaze fell to the ground. If he wasn't mistaken, she was holding back her tears. "I only hope my father will get here before the High Sheriff returns to marry me."

"Marry you?" Jacob turned her around to look in her eyes. "What are you talking about? No wedding banns have been posted and you told me you'd never marry the man."

"Sir Gregory said he doesn't care that I have the power to agree to a marriage or not. It sounded as if he were going to get King Richard to renege my privilege from me. That's why he left to fetch the bishop. He said when he returns, the bishop is going to marry us right away."

"The wretched cur," spat Jacob, pulling her closer. He had thought the High Sheriff went to get the bishop for the cele-bration of St. Catherine's Day. But now, it seemed as if there would be a celebration that was a marriage instead. He hugged Maira and looked over her head, devising a plan to beat the High Sheriff at his own game. "There is a way we can keep that from happening, even if your father doesn't show up in time."

"How can we do that?" Maira looked up in question, her glassy eyes reflecting the sky above them. "We have no power to stop him, or the wedding."

"Then let the church do it instead," he said.

"I don't understand what you mean."

"My brother is a priest, Maira. His church is only two hours' ride from here. We can beat the High Sheriff at his own game."

"Jacob, what are you suggesting?"

"If you're already married when the High Sheriff returns, there is nothing he can do about it."

"Already married?" she gasped.

Jacob nodded. "It can be done tomorrow morning, before the High Sheriff returns to Durham Castle." He bent down on one knee, holding Maira's hands in his. This was a risk, but one worth taking. "Lady Maira, will you marry me and become my wife?"

CHAPTER 14

"Marry you?" At first Maira thought Jacob was jesting. But when she saw the look on his face, she realized he was serious. "Get up, Jacob. Please."

"Not until you agree to be my wife." He still held her hands and stared intensely into her eyes, waiting for her answer. Although she felt attracted to Jacob and would much rather marry him than the High Sheriff, she kept thinking what her father or the earl who had been her guardian would say. "My father and the earl want an alliance with the High Sheriff," she told him.

"They won't still want you to be betrothed to him after they find out what a wretched man he is."

Maira had no doubt her father would be furious and her mother would cry if she came home married to a man who was naught more than a thief. "I don't know," said Maira. "I'm not sure my parents or my guardian would like it if I married you."

"What does it matter what they think?" he asked her. "You said you were granted permission by the late king to choose your own husband. So you can choose to marry me. Do it now before the High Sheriff returns and tells you that you no longer have that power."

"It's not that simple," she explained. "I wasn't really granted permission to choose a husband . . . just the permission to agree or disagree to a betrothal."

Jacob's smile faded and he slowly got to his feet. "Then you agreed to the betrothal with the High Sheriff before you came to Durham?"

"Nay, I didn't. I disagreed to it."

"If you disagreed to it . . . then why are you even here?"

"I told my father I'd give the High Sheriff a fortnight. If I didn't feel the marriage between us would work, then I would be able to go home."

"Then you want to marry the High Sheriff?"

"Nay! Of course not."

"Then you want to marry me."

"I – I don't know. I told you that I don't think my parents would like me getting married before I told them about it."

"Oh, I see," he said with a slight nod. His jaw clenched and his words were forced. "You don't feel I'm worthy of marrying you since your grandfather was the king and I no longer hold a title or lands."

"Well, you were excommunicated," she said, not looking at him when she spoke.

"From the church, not from being able to marry. Besides, all that is going to change once I attack and seize Durham Castle."

"Jacob, as much as I want you to be lord of Durham Castle, it isn't that easy to reverse an excommunication. It might take months or even years, and we don't have the time."

"That's why we'll get married right here in the woods," said Jacob with a wave of his hand through the air."

"I am a noblewoman," she reminded him. "When I someday marry, it has to be in a church as is proper."

"Or what?" he challenged her.

"What do you mean?" Maira felt scared for one of the first times in her life. Everything was happening so quickly.

"You don't seem to me like a woman who is afraid of what others think of her."

"I'm not."

"You come across as a rebel."

"I'm not a rebel. You don't know me if you think I'm rebellious in any way."

"Mayhap, you're the one who doesn't know yourself, Maira." He turned and started back to the horse.

"Wait," she cried. "Why are you walking away in the middle of our conversation?" She followed after him quickly.

"This conversation is over." He slid his hands around her waist and hoisted her up atop the horse. "It's obvious you don't want to marry me so there is nothing more to say."

"But I never said I wouldn't marry you," she protested as he pulled himself up behind her and turned the horse.

"Neither did you say you would. I don't have time for games, Sweetheart. I have an army to finish training and a job to do. I've already been too distracted by you. When we get back to camp, I think it is best if you take Ricker and leave."

"Leave?" Maira's heart skipped a beat. "But what about the rest of the training? Should I return early tomorrow? I want to help."

"If you want to help, then stay at the castle and hide with the boy in the tunnels until after the attack."

"Hide? I'm not going to hide. I'm going to fight alongside you just like you wanted."

"I changed my mind. I don't want you to fight in my army anymore."

"Why not?" she asked, feeling rejected. "You know I can fight better than any of the villagers."

"Nay, Maira," he said, getting back to camp and dismounting quickly. "I made a mistake in asking you to fight, and even a bigger mistake in asking you to marry me. Go back to Durham Castle and marry the High Sheriff like your father and guardian want you to do. And when you're a widow left alone to raise a child that isn't even of your womb, don't blame me for doing what I had to do."

"What you had to do?" asked Maira, dismounting his horse by herself. "What does that mean? Are you talking about killing the High Sheriff?"

"That's exactly what I mean. I have decided I will kill the man no matter if you are married to him or not. So don't even ask me to change my mind because I won't."

"Stop it, Jacob. You are acting like some sort of . . . assassin."

"Aye, I suppose that's what I'll be once I carry my plan through. I'll be a rebellious, excommunicated thief and assassin. I can see why you don't want to marry me. Now go."

He turned and stormed away, disappearing into his tent. Will walked up with Ricker in his arms. The boy clung to the wooden wolf Jacob had carved for him. He started crying, looking for Jacob.

"Shall I take the boy back to Jacob so he'll stop crying?" asked Will.

"Nay," she said, taking Ricker from him, glaring at the tent.

"Let Jacob cry. He deserves it. No one can talk to me that way."

"Jacob? Oh, no, I meant to stop the boy from crying," said Will with a chuckle.

"I know what you said, and I meant what I said as well," replied Maira, heading for her horse. "Jacob will cry when I'm married to the High Sheriff. And you can tell him that I'm going to reveal his plan as soon as Sir Gregory returns." She mounted her horse and headed out of camp with the crying boy on her lap, feeling as if she were the one who was going to cry next.

JACOB POKED his head out of the tent as Maira and the boy rode away through the woods.

"Roger," he called to one of the village men who he knew he could rely on.

"Aye, my lord," said Roger, hurrying to his side with a sword in his hand.

"Take Gerald with you and follow Lady Maira. Make certain she and the boy get back to the castle unharmed."

"We'll do that," said Roger, hurrying away.

"Will, fetch my horse quickly," Jacob said next.

"My lord?" asked Will in question. "Are we going somewhere this late in the day?"

"We're not, but I am." Jacob grabbed his cloak from the tent and continued to don it as he spoke. "I probably won't be back until the morning, so I'm counting on you to handle things at camp."

"You know you can count on me, my lord. But may I ask where you are going?"

"I'm going to Hartlepool."

"Hartlepool? On the coast?" asked Will. "That's a good two hour ride from here. Why are you going there?"

"Lady Maira said she was going to reveal our plan to Sir Gregory and I can't let her do that."

"So . . . shouldn't you be going to Durham Castle instead of Hartlepool then?"

"Nay. My brother is in Hartlepool and, right now, he is the only one who can possibly help me out of this mess."

"Oh, he's going to fight with us." Will nodded as if the idea pleased him. "We could always use another hand."

"Nay, he's going to marry Maira and me." Just as Jacob was preparing to mount his horse, his eye caught on something shining in the sun. It was Maira's sword, still lying on the rock where he had placed it before he took her to the knoll. His heart ached that she had rejected him, but this was no time to mourn his loss. The High Sheriff was returning to Durham tomorrow and there was no way in hell Jacob was going to let the bastard marry Maira. He knew Maira didn't want Sir Gregory. The man was naught but a murderer and a thief. Jacob left her sword where it was and mounted his horse, realizing he would be naught but a murderer and a thief once he killed the High Sheriff and stole the castle. Then again, Jacob didn't care.

He would bring his brother back with him. And once he convinced Maira that he was going to be a titled nobleman again someday soon, she would marry him without hesitation. If that didn't work . . . he didn't know what the hell he was going to do.

CHAPTER 15

*M*aira rode back to the castle as fast as she could, trying to keep Ricker quiet, but he kept crying. As she neared the end of the forest path, she was sure she heard hoofbeats following her. Glancing over her shoulder she could see two riders in the distance. Although she couldn't see them well, she was sure neither of them were Jacob. They wore dark cloaks and their heads were covered. As far as she knew, they could be bandits. With the boy's crying there would be no way to even hide.

She reached back for her sword to protect the child but, to her horror, it was missing. That's when she remembered that she had been so upset with Jacob that she left it back at his hidden camp. Well, there was no way she could retrieve it now. The sun had already set, and nightfall was upon her. The bandits were on her tail. There was nothing else she could do but to ride faster and get back to the castle before they caught up with her.

"Hold on to your doggie," she told Ricker, speaking of the carved wolf Jacob had made for him. Her arm closed around the boy tightly and she rode as fast as she could until she exited the woods. Glancing back, she was relieved to no longer see the riders. Entering the courtyard through the front gate, she didn't waste time trying to sneak in without being seen. Since the High Sheriff had yet to return, it didn't really matter.

"My lady," said Alf, rushing over to take the reins of her horse. Quickly, Maira slid off the horse with Ricker in her arms.

"If any of the guards ask where I've been, tell them I was taking Ricker for a ride through the fields to make him stop crying," Maira instructed.

"Aye, my lady." Alf took her horse to the stable while Maira hurried to the keep with Ricker in her embrace. When she entered the kitchen, she found Cleo and Tommy and the rest of the kitchen servants cleaning up the mess from the last meal.

"Lady Maira." Cleo dried her hands on a towel and threw it down. She rushed over and took the boy from her. "We were all getting worried about you. Some of the High Sheriff's guards were asking why you weren't at the main meal."

"Well, I'm back now."

"Lady Maira, your sword is missing," said Tommy pointing to the empty sheath on her back.

"Aye, it is," she answered. "Cleo, can you give Ricker something to eat?"

"Of course, my lady. Did you want me to keep him in my room off the kitchen tonight? He likes to play with the kittens that sleep on my bed."

"Thank you, I would like that," said Maira with a quick nod of her head.

"Can I fix you something to eat? There are a few leftovers."

"Thank you, but I'm not hungry, just tired," said Maira, leaving the kitchen and heading straight to her chamber. When she entered the room, she lit a candle and collapsed atop the bed. Then, being able to hold back her emotions no longer, she cried. Why had she not agreed to marry Jacob? Part of her wanted to be his wife. But another part of her feared what the High Sheriff would do to her or him when he found out. Not to mention, she feared what her father and the earl would say if they found out she married an excommunicated man who had been stripped of his title and had no castle or land to his name.

Maira had always thought of herself as a warrior. She had the natural instinct to want to protect those she loved and didn't think anything could frighten her. But today was different. Today, she felt shaken and unsure of herself and feared every little thing. It wasn't a good feeling because it made her weak. Crying into the pillow, exhausted, Maira drifted off to sleep. It wasn't long before she started dreaming of her late mentor, Imanie, once again.

"Maira, why on earth are you crying?" asked Imanie.

Maira dried her eyes, happy to see her mentor once again. She needed to talk to someone right now and perhaps Imanie's wisdom could guide her.

"I'm frightened, Imanie. I've never felt this way before."

The old woman cocked her head and looked at Maira with one eye closed. "This doesn't sound like you, Maira. You were always the strongest of the cousins. I've never known you to cry before. Do you want to tell me about it?"

"Everything is different since I met Jacob," she told the old woman with a sniffle.

"How so?"

"He wants to marry me, Imanie."

"And that made you cry?"

"Nay. I was crying because I never gave him an answer. I left him so quickly that I even forgot my sword."

"Ah," said Imanie with a chuckle. "I see it all clearly now."

"What do you see? Tell me."

"Only one thing could make you drop your tough exterior and cry like a babe in the seclusion of your chamber. You are in love with the man."

"In love?" Maira sat up. "I don't understand. Love wouldn't make me frightened and make me cry."

"Any man who can break that hardened exterior of yours enough that you left your sword behind must have some tremendous power over you. I've never known you to accidentally forget your weapon. Your blade is the thing that means the most to you."

"Aye," said Maira, calming enough to see things clearly now. "I thought my weapons meant the most to me, but now I'm not so sure."

"I saw you with little Ricker in your arms. You have a natural ability to always want to protect others. Even without your sword, you saw to protect the boy with no thought of yourself."

"I want to protect Jacob as well," she answered, rubbing her eyes. "But I don't know how to do that."

"Well, I don't think leaving him in the woods down on a bended knee giving his heart to you as you rode away is a way to protect him, do you?"

"Nay, I suppose it isn't." Maira thought of her actions and now regretted it. "I think I made a mistake, Imanie."

"Do what your heart, not your head tells you, Maira. That is the only way to be true to yourself. That is what makes a person strong."

"You're right, Imanie. Thank you for talking with me. I think I know now what I need to do."

She was pulled out of her dream when the door to her room burst open with a loud bang against the wall. Her eyes sprang open in alarm and she jumped off the bed, grabbing her dagger that was still attached to her waist belt. Her reactions were those of a warrior, always ready to defend. Steadily, she held the dagger out in front of her with both hands.

"Who goes there?" she shouted, no longer feeling frightened. The blood coursing through her made her feel brave and alive, just like it should be.

The silhouette of a woman stood in the doorway holding a lit candle. The woman brought the candle closer to her face for Maira to see her identity.

"Maira, it's me, Morag," said the girl, stepping into the room.

"Morag!" Maira dropped her dagger atop the bed and sighed a breath of relief. Rushing across the floor, she threw her arms around Morag in a big hug.

"Ye sure seem happy to see me, Cousin." Maira's action seemed to baffle Morag. Maira wasn't one to normally hug anyone.

"You have no idea how happy I am," explained Maira. "Where is Father?" She glanced out the door, scanning the darkened corridor. "You sure made good time. I didn't expect to see Father for at least another few days."

"I'm here with Branton only," Morag explained. "He took our wagon to the stable."

"Branton?" Maira's brows dipped and she started to get the

feeling something was wrong. "Wasn't my father at Whitehaven?"

"I dinna ken," Morag told her as Maira released her from the hug. "We never made it to Rothbury so I never had the chance to send a messenger to Whitehaven."

"What do you mean?" asked Maira in a low voice, feeling suddenly cold. "The plan was that you and Branton were to send a messenger to find Father and bring him back here to help me escape the wretched High Sheriff."

"Maira, we met up with ruffians on the road and had to turn back. Thank the Heaven's there were only two of them. Branton bravely fought them both off, and left them in a heap on the road."

"He did?" Suddenly, Maira felt as if she was being insensitive. The closer she looked at Morag, the more it verified that there had, indeed, been a struggle. Morag's gown was dirty and torn. Her hair was loose and disheveled. Morag always cared about her appearance, almost as much as their finicky cousin, Willow. She wouldn't be walking around looking like this unless something was amiss.

"We had to throw our trunks off the cart so we could make better time," Morag told her. "Oh, Maira, I was so frightened. I wished ye had been there to protect me." Morag fell into Maira's arms, almost dropping the candle. She wept bitterly, making Maira feel as if she had failed at doing the only thing at which she excelled. She should have been there to protect Morag and she wasn't. Now, she realized it had been selfish and foolish to send her cousin on a trip with just a young boy along for protection. At the time, Maira thought she was protecting her by sending her away. But now, she realized her mistake. She should have kept Morag near and paid close attention to her safety. Her foolish mistake almost got her cousin killed.

"I'm so sorry," said Maira, wrapping her arm around the girl's shoulders and leading her to the bed. "Now give me that candle and lie down and get a good night's rest. Everything is fine and, in the morning, things will be even better."

"It is nearly mornin' now," said Morag with a yawn. "Maira, we traveled for days. I swear I didna get any shut eye at all because I was so afeared. If ye had been with us, I wouldna have had to worry."

"Stay here and sleep," she told Morag. "I had no idea it was already so close to morning. When I return, I'll bring you some food and wine."

"Return? Where are ye goin'?" asked Morag with another yawn. "Maira, please dinna leave me."

"I know you're tired but there is something important I must do."

"What could ye need to do that is more important than stayin' with yer cousin in her time of need?"

Maira sighed. She couldn't leave without explaining things to Morag. She'd always been the protector of the four cousins and she wouldn't let the girl down. "I need to talk to someone, Morag. It's something very important. Can I trust you with a secret?"

"Secret?" Morag's half-closed lids sprang open wide and she sat up straight in bed. "Maira, ye are goin' to tell me a secret? Aye, I'd like to ken."

It was probably a mistake to tell Morag anything since she had already proven she couldn't keep her mouth shut. But Maira was distraught and had no one else to confide in besides the servants. What she had to say was something that only another girl her age could possibly understand.

"I am going to the woods to retrieve my sword. And I am also going there to meet Jacob. I will need you to help Cleo watch Ricker until I return."

"Jacob? The thief?" gasped Morag.

"Aye, Morag. But he is not a thief. Not really. He is a nobleman who has lost everything because of the High Sheriff."

"So why are you goin' to see him? It is dangerous to be sneakin' out into the woods to meet with a common thief."

"Please don't call Jacob a thief again."

"Well, that is what he is. Or did ye already forget that he stole weapons from Rothbury?"

"Nay, Morag, I didn't forget. But you mustn't forget that he is a man. A nobleman who doesn't deserve what he got. I am going to the woods to not only meet him, but also to marry him."

CHAPTER 16

*E*ven with Morag's protests, Maira listened to her heart like Imanie had told her to do. She made her way to the forest to meet with Jacob as the sun rose on the horizon. As she approached the camp, she was stopped right before she entered. Villagers appeared on the road all aiming their weapons at her.

"I come in peace," she said from the top of her horse, raising her hands in the air to show them she was not a threat.

"How do we know that for sure?" growled the man she recognized as Roger.

"Roger, it's me, Lady Maira," she told him, lowering her hood so he could see her face as well as her crown. Hopefully, seeing the crown would remind these people that she was the granddaughter of the late king. "Please tell Jacob I am here to retrieve my sword."

"He's not here," growled the villager named Gerald, holding a battle axe over his shoulder.

"Gerald, for Heaven's sake, have you forgotten that I am the one who helped train you? And didn't I tell you to never rest the axe over your shoulder? Hold it up steady with both hands and be ready to defend yourself at all times."

"You left us, or did you forget?" asked Will, walking through the crowd of men with a sword pointed at her as well.

"Will? You don't believe me that I mean no harm?" asked Maira.

"How do we know this isn't a trap?" asked Roger.

"That's right," added Will. "When you left here you said you were going to reveal our plan to the High Sheriff."

"I didn't mean it. I was just upset," she explained, feeling bad about her previous behavior. "Besides, I couldn't have told the High Sheriff because he's not even back from his trip yet."

Will whispered to the other men and then nodded. "All right. You are free to pass and retrieve your sword, but then you need to go."

"Nay, she will stay," came a voice from behind her as two riders approached.

"Jacob!" she cried, happy to see him again. Then she noticed that the man with him atop the other horse was a priest. "Is that your brother?" she asked curiously.

"Aye," said Jacob with a slight nod, stopping his horse in front of her. "This is my brother, Father Frank."

"Hello, nice to meet you," she said to the priest, wondering what he was doing here.

"Everyone back to camp immediately," Jacob commanded. "We have no time to waste. The High Sheriff will be returning tomorrow and there is a lot to be done before then."

"Can I help with more training while I'm here?" asked Maira, hoping Jacob wouldn't turn her away.

"Nay, not now," he said with no emotion at all on his face.

"Since you are here, it saves me the trouble of having to abduct you."

"Abduct me?" She shook her head and giggled nervously. "Jacob, what are you saying?"

"Maira, I am going to marry you, like it or not."

"What?" she asked in confusion, not liking this turn of events. "Jacob, you don't have to threaten me. I came here of my own accord to tell you I will marry you."

"You did?" That seemed to surprise him.

"Of course, I did. I am sorry for not accepting your proposal of marriage yesterday, but I was confused and scared."

"So what's changed?" he asked as they rode to camp.

"I listened to my heart instead of my head," she explained, knowing the best way to protect Jacob was to be his wife. "I think if we are married, then the plans to attack Durham can be canceled. If you are married to me, you can live as a nobleman as my husband. In time, I will speak with my cousin, the king, and ask him to talk to the pope. Hopefully, eventually, you can get the excommunication reversed."

"And what about the High Sheriff?" asked Jacob. "Are you suggesting I just let him get away with all the corrupt things he's done? Am I supposed to look the other way and let him keep the castle that should be mine?"

"I'll talk to Richard about it. He'll listen to me. I will ask Willow and Fia to help me. My cousins can be very persuasive. It'll work out, you'll see."

This was the best plan for all involved, thought Maira. She would be able to help Jacob and not only protect him but keep him and his army from dying needlessly. Aye, she had found a way to protect them all.

. . .

JACOB FELT like Maira had just driven a stake right through his heart. She expected him to back down and let the High Sheriff win this whole thing. Well, that was not going to happen.

"I will make no promises, Maira. But no matter what the outcome, my offer to marry you still holds true. I love you. But the question is, do you love me?"

"I – I think so," said Maira, not at all sounding confident with her answer. But at this point, he didn't have a choice. By marrying Maira, he would keep her from marrying Sir Gregory and living a miserable life. In the process, he would be stopping the High Sheriff from taking another of Jacob's brides.

"That's good enough," he said, sliding off his horse as they approached the camp. "Frank, I'll need you to marry us right away. There is no time to lose." He reached up and put his arms around Maira's waist and set her on the ground.

"Jacob, I am happy you finally came to terms with my decision to be a priest," said Frank. He was a tall, thin man with dark curly hair and eyes the same gray tone as Jacob's. "But tell me, Brother. Are you sure the reason you came to find me after all this time isn't only because you have a personal vendetta against the High Sheriff?"

Jacob wished his brother wouldn't have asked him this in front of Maira. Her head snapped around and her bright blue eyes scrutinized him as she, too, waited for his answer. He didn't want to lie to a priest. Part of Jacob's reasoning to bring Frank here was, indeed, to get back at Sir Gregory. But he also wasn't lying when he said he loved Maira. Even in the short

181

time that he'd known her, he had lost his heart to the fierce but petite lady.

"I told you, Frank, I love Maira. That is not a lie. Whether she loves me in return is yet to be determined."

"Do you love Jacob as well?" The priest turned his attention to Maira, taking the heat off of Jacob.

Maira suddenly became fidgety. "Father, I must admit that I have never known love with a man before, so I am confused on the matter."

"Do you feel an attraction to him? Do you think you can love him in time?" asked the priest.

Maira's eyes met Jacob's and he felt his heart flutter. No man wanted to be rejected. Jacob didn't know if he could accept it if she were to say she didn't love him and wasn't sure if she ever could. Will, as well as all of the villagers, stood around watching and listening. It made Jacob feel extremely uncomfortable. Jacob didn't want to hear her answer at this time and decided to intervene.

"Love is not a prerequisite for marriage and you know it, Brother," he told Frank. "Now, enough of this idle chatter. Where do you want us to stand for the wedding?"

"Right here is fine, I guess," said Frank, pulling his prayer book out from beneath his cloak. "I take it all these people will be witnesses to the marriage?"

"Aye, that's fine." Jacob wanted to move forward quickly before Maira changed her mind. He had never meant to abduct her or to force her to marry him. He only said it to sound strong around the villagers. He had, at one time, been the late Lord of Durham's Captain of the Guard. Men feared and respected him at the same time. Lady Catherine loved him. It was hard for a man to go from that to being a thief hiding away in the woods wondering where he'd find his next meal. He was neither feared nor respected anymore and, at times, his confidence even seemed to be dwindling. His pride was hurt and it ate away at him every day. He would do anything to regain what he'd once lost. But he only hoped Maira wouldn't hate him for it in the end.

BEFORE MAIRA KNEW what had happened, Father Frank was pronouncing her and Jacob husband and wife.

"It's a shame you don't have a ring," said Father Frank. "However, it isn't necessary. You may kiss the bride, Jacob."

Maira's heart beat rapidly in her chest as Jacob leaned over in front of everyone and placed his lips upon hers. It was at that moment that she realized listening to her heart was the right thing to do. With his tall frame towering over her, she felt safe and happy in his presence. Looking up into his eyes, she smiled.

"We're really married?" she whispered, barely able to say the words aloud. It had all happened so fast that she had no time to consider how she was going to tell her father about this. But with Jacob at her side, she was sure she could convince her father it was the right thing to do.

"We are," said Jacob, bending over and scooping her up in his arms.

"Jacob, what are you doing?" She felt her cheeks flush as everyone stared at them and clapped.

"There is still one item to attend to that will solidify the marriage."

"There is?" He headed to the tent, and that could only mean one thing.

"We need for the marriage to be consummated," he told her.

"Now?" She suddenly felt very nervous. She hadn't really thought much about this part. And she also never thought she'd lose her virginity in a tent in the woods either. She reached up and held her crown on her head as Jacob picked up his pace.

He bent over and entered the tent with her still in his arms. The flap to the tent closed behind him, blocking out the sun and leaving them in the semi-dark. As he kissed her passionately, she felt her body warming to his advances. He gently laid her down on a pallet that was covered with a soft blanket. There was one fluffy pillow there as well. For a pallet in a tent, Jacob knew how to be comfortable. She closed her eyes momentarily, feeling as if she were back in the castle, lying atop a plush bed surrounded by velvet curtains. She felt like a royal queen right now inside a castle instead of a rebellious bride marrying in secret in the middle of the forest.

"I'm sorry I didn't have time to get a ring," he told her, his deep, sultry voice causing her to open her eyes. He had already removed his shoes and was unbuckling his weapon belt. He was almost too tall for the tent as his head scraped against the ceiling. "I promise you, when this is all over and I have money again someday, I'll buy you the grandest ring you've ever seen."

"It's not important," she said in a small shaky voice, suddenly feeling very shy.

He quickly removed his tunic and breeches and stood before her in only his braies. The sun outside lit up the sides of the tent giving an orange glow to his skin. His chest looked broad and sturdy and his nipples were dark and flat with raised bumps in the middle. Her eyes roamed from his hand-some face, down his chest and to his torso. His fingers fumbled with the ties on his braies. Mesmerized, she couldn't look away.

"I hope you'll like what you see," he muttered, dropping his braies and exposing his aroused form. His long, thick shaft looked hard and ready for making love. She gasped, never having seen an aroused and naked man before.

"I – I . . ." She had no idea how to respond and kept staring at his engorged form. It made her feel randy.

"I think it's time you remove some of these clothes, Wife."

His use of the word wife and his naked body pressing up against her as he removed her crown made her realize that this was for real. "This is nice," he said, inspecting the crown and putting it down beside the pallet. "I'm surprised the High Sheriff didn't take it from you."

She almost got upset that he'd mentioned the High Sheriff at a time like this, but forgot all about it when his hands brushed against the top of her breasts as he untied the laces of her bodice. "Sit up," he instructed, helping her as he pushed the gown off her shoulders and unbuckled her belt and removed her weapons as well as her gown. Her shoes and hose followed. And then he slid his hands up her bare legs, leaning over and kissing her as he expertly removed her braies. Little by little, he pulled her shift up over her body, only stopping his kisses so he could bring it up and over her head. Then he threw her shift to the floor, kneeling next to her, perusing her naked body.

"By the Rood, you are perfect and ever so beautiful." His breathing deepened, making his chest move in and out. "I'm almost afraid to touch you for fear you'll break."

"You needn't be afraid, I won't break," she assured him and smiled.

"You are so fierce yet so tiny that it amazes me, Maira."

Mayhap she should have been frightened, but Jacob's presence made her feel so aroused that all she could think about was how it would feel once he entered her.

"Jacob," she said, wetting her dry lips with her tongue. "I have never done this before. I'll need you to instruct me."

"There's naught to worry about my angel." As he kissed her gently on the lips, one of his hands slid slowly up her side and cupped one of her breasts. Then he repeated the action with his other hand, cupping her mounds and squeezing slightly. "Just relax and let your heart guide you."

When his mouth covered one nipple and his tongue shot out to circle it, she arched up off the bed. A bolt of energy shot through her. She could feel vibrating all the way down between her legs.

"Do you like that?" he asked her, letting his hand slide down her torso and to her waist.

"I do," she whispered, starting to feel a fire burning in her belly. And when he cupped her womanly mound and used the tips of his fingers to tease her, she just about shot off the bed.

"I need to ready you before I enter so it won't hurt."

"All right," she said, not sure what he meant by that but also no longer caring. Her eyes traveled lower and rested on his manhood once again.

"Give me your hand," he said, reaching out to take it.

"What for?" she asked, feeling naïve with his next action. He guided her hand to his stiff shaft and closed her fingers around it. "Oh!" she cried out.

"Play with that for a while," he mumbled. "Stroke me as I

stroke you."

She did as he suggested, and found herself relaxing until she felt one of his fingers slip inside her. She jerked slightly in surprise.

"Did I hurt you?" he asked, as if he really cared. She liked that. Even though he was ready to burst, he cared about her comfort.

"Nay, it was just a surprise," she told him as he thrust his finger in and out, guided by the liquid of love.

"I think you're ready," he said, spreading her legs and settling himself in between them. "I promise to be gentle," he told her. "And I want you to promise to let loose."

"Me?" she asked through ragged breaths. "What do you mean?"

"If you feel yourself wanting more, then say so. If you feel like screaming out in passion, I don't want you to hold back."

"Scream out? Whatever for?"

He cocked a sly smile and ran a loving hand along her cheek. "You will hopefully never have to ask that again by the time we are done."

"All right," she said, feeling a little apprehensive. Her eyes darted around the tent, wondering if anyone was going to enter.

"No one will disturb us," he assured her as if he could read her mind. "Now, close your eyes and just bask in the pleasure you are about to feel."

"Close my eyes?" she asked, not sure she wanted to miss a thing.

"Shhh, it's all right," he told her, moving between her thighs and reaching up to kiss her lips at the same time. "Just enjoy it."

He kissed and caressed her for a few more minutes and then she felt the tip of his hardened manhood at her door. Jacob was extremely patient and took his time to slip into her little by little, waiting to make sure she was comfortable before he continued.

"I can feel you in me," she whispered, excited to finally be coupling with a man. She hadn't thought she wanted this, but now it was all she could think of.

"Don't talk. Just . . . feel." He slid his entire length into her then. At first it felt tight and as if he'd broken through a barrier. Then, with his soft kisses and caressing, she relaxed and felt something she wasn't expecting at all. With each gentle thrust, he glided in and out, bringing her to life. It was as if he found a secret button to push and when he did, she felt herself liking the action and longing for more.

"Oooh," she moaned aloud, keeping her eyes closed all the while.

"You like that?"

"I do."

His hands slid around to her rear end and he guided her to move her hips as their bodies met in unbridled passion.

"Maira," he whispered, his actions becoming faster.

"Jacob," she answered, feeling more and more excited. Here was her husband, arousing her and bringing her to ecstasy with every thrust. And then she felt like her body was acting on its own as she met him in the dance of life and love.

A vibrating sensation became stronger between her thighs, the thought of him being one with her making her cry out in elation.

She moaned. He moaned, too. And then as if they belonged

together, with their bodies joined as one, she found her release.

"Oh, Jacob!" she cried out. "Ooooh."

Colors flashed behind her closed lids and she was brought to the brink and then fell over the edge. As if he'd been waiting for her to be satisfied, he held out for as long as he could. Then she shouted loudly like some kind of beast as he released his seed into her.

"Aaaaaah. Damn this feels good," he shouted so loudly that Maira was sure everyone heard him, but he didn't care. Then he collapsed next to her, holding her tightly in his arms. Only the sound of their breathing filled the tent.

"Have we consummated the marriage?" she asked, just to be sure.

He started laughing and pulled her atop him, kissing her on the head. "Aye, my rebellious little angel. The deed is done. We are now married in every way."

She smiled as she snuggled up to his chest and closed her eyes, listening to his rapidly beating heart. It felt good to be married, although she never thought it would. Now, because they were man and wife, she had protected Jacob and possibly saved his life.

"We can go back to Rothbury or to Whitehaven now," she told him.

"Whatever for?"

She opened her eyes and lifted her head. "We can live there until you regain your title. I'm sure I can talk either the earl or my father into letting us stay at one of their castles."

"We won't need to," he said, staring up at the ceiling. "We'll live at Durham Castle where we belong."

"What?" She slowly sat up and looked down at him "Jacob?

What are you saying? You're not still thinking of going through with the attack are you?"

"Of course I am. Why wouldn't I?"

She scowled at him. "Because we're married now. You don't need to attack Durham. I'll go back and get Morag and Branton and we can leave for Whitehaven before the High Sheriff returns."

"You're suggesting I run? How could you? I never expected that from someone like you." He sat up and stared at her, making her feel like some kind of traitor. "Just because we're married, it changes nothing. I am still going to attack Durham Castle and take back what should have rightfully been mine."

"Nay!" she shouted, getting up and putting on her clothes as well as donning her crown. "You don't need to do that anymore now that we're married. You promised."

"I promised nothing," he growled, getting dressed as well.

She thought back to what he'd said earlier and realized that what he told her was true. He never did promise not to stop his plans once they were married. Perhaps, it was only wishful thinking on her part that he would.

"I can't believe this," she spat, strapping on her weapons. "I am going to be a widow because you're going to get yourself killed."

"How little confidence you have in me, Maira. That hurts. But nay, I promise you I won't die but I can't say the same thing for the High Sheriff."

"Jacob this is insanity. Now stop this nonsense and come back to Whitehaven with me. My father will help you regain your title."

"I don't want or need his help. I will do this on my own." He finished dressing and strapped on his sword. "Now, you will stay here until after the attack on the morrow. We are moving in when the High Sheriff sends most of his men out on the hunt. It's the only day he's allowed to hunt in the king's forest so he takes advantage of it. He is greedy and that's why he sends more men than he should. I will sneak in with my army through the tunnels and before he knows what happened, I'll be Lord of Durham and he'll be dead. With a little luck, I'll be able to claim the title of High Sheriff as well."

"You disgust me," she said, feeling now that mayhap she'd made a mistake in marrying him.

"What do you mean?" He honestly looked as if he had no idea what she was talking about.

"You fed me the lie of loving me so I'd marry you just so you could get what you wanted."

"You're not making any sense, Maira. I do love you. And now that you're my wife, I am going to protect you. I don't want you anywhere near the fighting during the attack, do you understand?"

"I thought you asked me to fight with you against the High Sheriff."

"I changed my mind."

"Well, mayhap I didn't. Where is my sword? I demand you return it to me at once."

"It's right there," he said with a nod. "Feel free to take it. But you still won't be fighting with me during the attack." She turned to find her sword lying on the ground in a dark corner. She picked it up and headed out the door, bumping into Will and Father Frank. Everyone was crowded around the tent, watching and listening. Then Will started clapping and the rest followed suit.

"Congratulations," said Will. "We all heard the consummation and can vouch that the union has been finalized."

"Nothing is final," she spat, glaring at Jacob who emerged from the tent. "If you all want to risk your lives attacking Durham Castle and going up against the High Sheriff and his trained men, then don't let me stop you. But I won't be a part of this suicide mission. Nay. I will not stand by and watch innocent people die because of the stubbornness of one hard-headed fool."

"If you mean me, then just come out and say it," said Jacob.

"All right, I mean you Jacob Quincey. Because of your pride, these innocent villagers are going to die."

There were mumbles of concern amongst the men. Jacob stormed over to her and took her by the elbow.

"Maira," he said in a low voice so only she could hear him. "Don't do this. I have worked too hard to throw it all away now. I am so close to getting everything I want. I don't need you putting doubt into the heads of my men at this point. Now, stop it."

"Let go of me," she retorted, pulling out of his hold and mounting her horse.

"Where are you going?" he demanded to know.

"I am going back to Durham Castle to get my cousin, Morag, and Branton. Then we are leaving and going back to Whitehaven with or without you."

"Maira, stay. You are my wife now."

"Not for long."

"What does that mean?" he asked.

"It means I will be a widow come the morrow and now I regret ever having married you at all, Jacob Quincey." Maira rode back to the castle holding back her tears. She refused to be weak or to ever cry again.

CHAPTER 17

*A*s soon as Maira approached the castle, she knew something was wrong. There were too many guards on the wall walk, not to mention that the tension in the courtyard could be felt hanging thick in the air.

"Maira!" Morag hurried across the courtyard toward her, holding the hand of little Ricker. The boy gripped on to the carved wolf that Jacob had given him. Branton appeared from the stable, taking the reins of her horse.

"Morag? I thought you'd be sleeping," said Maira.

"How could I, Cousin?" Morag looked tired but also very concerned. "The High Sheriff returned an hour ago and has been askin' for ye."

"He did?" Panic flowed through her. She scanned the courtyard, looking for him. "He wasn't supposed to return until the morrow."

"He brought the Bishop of Durham with him," said Branton. "He is telling everyone that he's marrying you at the St. Catherine's Day festival, right after the hunt."

"Oh, nay, he can't," she told them with a shake of her head.

"He says the king gave him permission and he even has a missive with the crown's stamp on it to prove it," Branton informed her.

"Oh, no." Maira's heart lodged in her throat. This wasn't good news at all.

"That's right," said Morag. "Our cousin betrayed ye, Maira. Richard said his late father's order of grantin' ye the right to choose yer husband no longer holds true."

"He can't do this," she said defiantly, not wanting to believe it.

"Well, he did," stated Morag.

"Nay, you don't understand." Maira felt trapped and doomed and as if she'd put everyone in danger. "Morag, Branton, don't say anything to the High Sheriff yet, but Jacob and I are married."

"Married?" exclaimed Morag. "I thought I told ye no' to do it."

"That might not have been a good idea," agreed Branton, making a face.

"I listened to my heart," she told them. "I thought if we were married, Jacob would forget about his attack on the castle. But it seems as if he is going through with it after all."

"Shhh, Maira. Dinna say anythin' in front of the boy." Morag nodded toward Ricker.

"It's all right," said Maira, patting Ricker's head. "He doesn't talk."

"Doggie," said Ricker, holding up the carved animal.

"Then what do you call that?" asked Branton.

"It's the only word he says." Maira picked up Ricker and gave him a hug. She had grown fond of the boy and didn't want to see him hurt in the attack. Sir Gregory didn't deserve to be the father of such a cute boy. It seemed such a shame and she felt sorry for Ricker. She would take measures to keep the boy from being punished by his father again. "Morag, I want you and Branton to take Ricker and leave here immediately. I'll warn the servants to stay in the tunnels during the attack."

"Take Ricker? Isna that stealin' a child?" asked Morag.

"Not if I'm protecting his life, it's not," answered Maira.

"What about you?" asked Branton. "Where will you be?"

"I'm going to stay here and fight."

"Fight? I dinna understand. Are ye fightin' for the High Sheriff?" asked Morag in surprise.

"Nay, Morag. I am going to fight to keep my husband alive, no matter what it takes to do it."

"Well, I'm no' leavin' again without ye. I'll help fight," offered Morag bravely.

"Me, too," added Branton. "Since I fought off the two bandits in the woods, I feel as if I have a lot more confidence now."

"This isn't the same," said Maira. "You don't understand. People are going to die. And we might have to kill in order to save our own lives or the lives of each other."

"I'm willing to do that," said Branton. "After all, a squire risks his life to protect his lord. That is his duty. This is no different. I want to be a squire someday, so this is good practice."

"What about you?" Maira asked Morag.

"I dinna ken how to fight," admitted Morag. "But I will do anythin' I can to help ye."

"If you two insist on staying then we'll need to come up with a plan." Maira paced back and forth, thinking, with the boy in her arms. "I'll let the servants know what is going on and, mayhap, they can help us."

"How can ye trust the servants? They might tell the High Sheriff," Morag pointed out.

"Cleo, the cook, is a member of the Followers of the Secret Heart," Maira told them.

"She is?" asked Morag, her hand covering her heart brooch on her bodice as she spoke.

"We'll tell her and she'll know who we can trust." Maira informed them. "But for now, we need to keep Sir Gregory away from me and from trying to marry me before the attack."

"That willna be easy," said Morag. "The man seems to always get what he wants."

"We'll have to tell the servants to help us then." Maira looked around the courtyard, spying Tommy. "I'll have them watch from the secret tunnels and we'll know every minute of the day what the High Sheriff is doing. Take Ricker and go back to my solar." Maira handed the little boy to Morag. "I'll get Tommy, Cleo, and Alf and we'll come through the passageway to meet you in a few minutes. Then we'll lay out our plan."

* * *

"Why did you let your wife leave without trying to stop her?" asked Father Frank.

Jacob sparred angrily with Will, taking out his frustration. "Lady Maira is a rebel. If you tell her one thing, she'll do the other. I had hoped by letting her go, she would have turned around and come back on her own by now."

"The day is nearly over and she hasn't returned," Will pointed out. "Perhaps she isn't coming."

"Dammit, Squire, I can see that and I don't need you to point it out." Jacob thrust angrily at Will, flipping the boy's sword out of his hand.

Will held his hands up over his head in surrender. "I'm unarmed, my lord. There is no need to keep fighting."

"I'm sorry, Will." Jacob bent over and picked up Will's sword and handed it to him. He looked over to the rest of the villagers who were practicing their fighting techniques, eager to help him overtake the High Sheriff. Was he really being selfish as Maira said? The villagers all knew the risk and still wanted vengeance against the man as well. Or did they? If they were only doing it because Jacob talked them into it, he wouldn't know what to think. After all, there was a good chance that they wouldn't make it out of this alive.

Jacob watched as some of the villagers' wives and children visited camp to see the progress. They were all innocent pawns in this very dangerous game. These children might lose their fathers. The women might lose their husbands. They had so little in life but were willing to risk it all just to help Jacob. How could he not have seen this before? It wasn't easy to think of what might happen. Maira was right. It was a suicide mission and he couldn't let these poor villagers lose their lives because of his vendetta against the High Sheriff.

"Tell the villagers the attack is called off." Jacob jammed his sword back into the scabbard.

"My lord?" asked Will in question. "What are you saying?"

"You heard me, Will. It's over. These people are not trained warriors. I don't know what I was thinking asking them to go up against skilled soldiers. I can't let them do it. I can't take the risk that they'll lose everything just so I can gain back what I lost."

"You're going to just give up after all this time?" asked Will. "That doesn't sound like you. I know how much you want your name cleared and your title restored, my lord. How can you let that all go?"

"How can I continue when I'm about to lose more than all of that put together?"

"I don't understand, my lord. What will you be losing?"

"If I go ahead with the attack, too many people will die. And because of my stubbornness and my selfishness, I will lose the woman I love. I will lose my wife in the process, and that is something I am not willing to give up for anything in the world."

CHAPTER 18

Maira opened the secret door in her bedchamber to allow Cleo, Alf and Tommy to enter. "Hurry," she told them, peeking down the passageway and then closing the door behind them.

"What is this all about?" asked Cleo. "Tommy said you wanted to see me. Is something wrong?"

"I'm married," she blurted out, watching the expression on Cleo's face.

"So . . . you already married the High Sheriff?" Cleo sounded very confused. "But he just returned. When did it happen?"

"She married the thief named Jacob," announced Morag.

"Morag!" Maira scolded her for telling.

"Oops." Morag covered her mouth with her hand. "Well, ye were about to tell her anyway, werena ye?"

"Aye, I was," Maira said with a sigh. "Cleo, Sir Jacob is planning an attack on Durham Castle when the High Sheriff sends his men out on the hunt. I am going to help him take back what Sir Gregory has stolen from him."

199

"My lady," said Cleo in surprise. "How is Sir Jacob going to fight everyone by himself?"

"He has trained some of the villagers and raised a small army. They are going to fight with him."

"Nay, they'll be slaughtered," protested Cleo, looking horrified by the thought. "You have to stop him."

"I tried, but his decision is made. As his wife, the only thing to do is to support him. Therefore, I am going to help him from inside the castle walls."

"I don't like this," said Cleo, shaking her head.

"Neither do I," admitted Maira. "But I decided I would do anything to help Jacob. He has had everything stolen from him and he was framed for the murder of the bishop when it wasn't his fault."

"The servants all like Sir Jacob, and we believe he is innocent," said Cleo. "I will talk to the rest of them and we will help in any way we possibly can."

"Can I fight with a sword?" asked Tommy excitedly.

"Nay!" snapped his mother, pulling him closer.

Maira looked down to Tommy's bare feet feeling bad that she still hadn't found him a pair of shoes. "Tommy, you and Alf will be our lookouts," she told him.

"I can do that," said Alf eagerly. "What do we have to do?"

"Keep a close eye on the High Sheriff and report back to me if he is doing anything suspicious."

"Someone's coming," announced Branton, peeking out the chamber door.

"Fast, everyone back into the tunnel." Maira hustled the servants and Branton into the tunnel and quickly closed the secret door. She had just finished when the High Sheriff entered the room, standing there with his hands on his hips.

"Where the hell have you been?" the man growled.

"I was taking care of Ricker," said Maira, nodding to the boy playing with his wooden animal on the bed. Morag sat next to him.

"What's that?" snapped the man, stomping into the room and walking over to the bed. He snatched up the wooden animal and inspected it. "Where did this come from?"

Maira's heart stood still. Ricker reached out for the animal and, to her horror, he said something she didn't want to hear.

"Jacob," said the boy, reaching for the wooden animal. "Doggie."

"Jacob?" Sir Gregory spun around and threw the wooden animal to the floor. It broke into several pieces. Ricker started crying. Morag pulled him onto her lap to calm him. "You were with the thief, just like I thought."

"He's not a thief," she said, knowing it was no use in denying the fact at this point.

"You will not leave this room until the wedding, do you understand me?"

"I can't marry you, my lord," she said bravely, hoping she wasn't doing the wrong thing.

"You can and you will. I have a missive from the king and he gives me his permission to marry you. You no longer have any say so in the matter."

"I cannot marry you because I'm already married. To Jacob." She held her breath and rested her hand atop the hilt of her dagger. Ricker cried louder, only infuriating the man.

"You lie!" he spat. "You have not married him. You will marry me."

"I assure you, I am already married and cannot marry you, my lord."

"Prove it," he snarled. "If you are married to that traitor, then where is he?"

"He's . . . not here."

"Of course he's not. And as soon as he and his makeshift little army arrives, they will be surprised to meet with the end of the swords of my army instead."

"What do you mean?" asked Maira, hoping beyond measure that he didn't know about the attack.

"I am not stupid." He shouted to be heard over Ricker's bawling. "I know Jacob is planning to attack when I send my men on the hunt tomorrow. But he and his army will all be surprised when they find out my soldiers are still here. They will die. Every single one of them will die for being so stupid. And you will marry me one way or another, I promise you that."

"Nay. Don't hurt them. Most of them are only villagers," she told him. "They are no threat to you."

"I know all about it, and I don't care. You, as well as the boy and your cousin, will be locked in this room and not let out until I have slayed your secret lover. I cannot believe you betrayed me!" His hand shot out and he hit Maira on the face. Immediately, she drew her dagger, but Sir Gregory was pulling Ricker off the bed and holding him with one arm as the boy kicked and squirmed, trying to get away. "Don't pull your blade on me unless you want to die as well," snarled the man heading to the door with the crying boy under his arm.

"Where are you taking Ricker?"

"Don't worry about it. He's my son. I am going to shut the whelp up and teach him not to cry."

"Please, don't hurt him. He's only a child."

Sir Gregory stopped and turned around. "Mayhap you

should have thought of that before you snuck him away to meet with Jacob. If anything happens to Ricker, it is on your head now."

"Nay, leave the boy alone," she said, rushing forward with her blade gripped tightly in her hand. Morag shot up off the bed and grabbed her arm to stop her.

"Nay, Maira. Dinna anger him more," she said under her breath.

"Guard, lock them in the room and don't let them out for anything," Sir Gregory ordered his man. "Stay watch at their door in case they try to escape."

"Aye, m'lord," said the guard, closing the door. Maira heard him turning the key in the lock.

"Nay!" shouted Maira, flinging her dagger at the door. The blade stuck in the wood, wavering back and forth.

"Dinna worry," Morag told her. "We have the tunnel and can still escape."

"Aye," said Maira, rushing over and opening the secret door. "Come on, Morag. We can no longer stay here."

"Where are we goin'?" asked Morag, rushing after her.

"We need to sneak out of here because we have to warn Jacob."

Maira led the way as they sneaked through the tunnel. Without a candle, they had to walk slowly. Morag was frightened in the dark and Maira had to hold her hand.

"Lady Maira," came a voice from up ahead.

"Tommy? Is that you?" asked Maira.

"Aye," said the boy. He came around the corner with a candle in his hand. "I wanted to report that the High Sheriff just went into his solar to meet with the Bishop of Durham. One of the other servants told me he overheard the bishop telling a guard he had something important to tell Sir Gregory that had to do with Lady Catherine."

"Lady Catherine?" asked Maira curiously. "I wonder what he has to say."

"You can listen at the peephole and find out," said the boy.

"Maira, I'm scared," said Morag. "I dinna want the High Sheriff to find us in the tunnels. If so, he will hit us."

"Don't be frightened," said Maira, putting her hand to her bruised cheek. "But perhaps it is better if I go to spy by myself. Morag, go back to the room and wait for me there. If you stay inside the room, there is no reason for the High Sheriff to get angry with you."

"I canna make it back to the room by myself. I'll get lost. Come with me, Maira."

"Nay. I need to find out what is going on, and I need to get a message to Jacob to warn him."

"I can sneak out of the castle and go to the woods to warn him," offered Tommy.

Maira thought of the last time the boy had tried to follow her. He was put in the pillory. Plus, he didn't even own a pair of shoes so he couldn't run if he had to.

"Nay, it's too dangerous. Tommy, take Morag back to the bedchamber. Then go to the kitchen and tell your mother that the High Sheriff knows about Jacob's plan."

"He does? That's not good," said the boy.

"Also, tell her that Sir Gregory took Ricker but I am going to get him back."

"Aye, my lady."

"Maira, where will ye be?" asked Morag. "Dinna forget me here. I'm frightened."

"Don't worry, Morag. Just stay in the room and you'll be safe. I've got work to do and will come back to get you later."

Maira sent Tommy with the candle to guide Morag back to the bedchamber. Things were getting complicated and she felt it was her job to keep everyone safe. But how could she do this and at the same time manage to warn Jacob not to attack? There were so many lives at stake, and only she could stop the massacre from happening.

She remembered the way to the High Sheriff's solar and stopped in front of the peephole in the wall. Hearing muffled voices from inside, she quietly popped out the cork that let her see into the room. She gasped when she saw Ricker in the room as well as the High Sheriff and the Bishop of Durham. The little boy was silent but there was a raised purple bruise over one eye.

"That bastard! If Jacob doesn't kill him, I will," she said to herself, wanting the High Sheriff to get what he deserved. Any man who purposely hurt a child – especially his own son – had to be addled.

"What is it you want?" snapped the High Sheriff, putting Ricker in a cage at the far side of the room and locking him inside. Ricker threw himself down, hiding his face and sobbing into his arms.

Maira couldn't believe what she was witnessing. Sir Gregory was a horrible man.

"My lord, is it necessary to lock the boy in a cage?" asked the bishop.

"He's my son and I'll do what I please. He will stay there until he learns not to cry." Sir Gregory walked over and poured himself a goblet of wine, chugging it down. He never offered any to the bishop.

"That's what I wanted to talk to you about," said the bishop, keeping his eye on the boy.

"Spit it out. What do you have to say?" asked the High Sheriff, pouring himself another goblet of wine.

"It's about the day Lady Catherine passed away.

"Lady Catherine?" Sir Gregory put down the goblet and picked up from the table the jeweled dagger that he'd taken from Maira. He caressed it and stroked it as he spoke. "I want her back," he said. "What do you have to tell me about her?"

"It's about her last confession, right before she died."

"Really?" The High Sheriff's eyebrows rose. "I thought confessions were supposed to be kept a secret."

"Usually they are. And I have kept this secret since her death, but I just can't keep it anymore." The bishop's eyes darted over to Ricker again.

"Go ahead." The High Sheriff gently put the dagger on the table and picked up the goblet and took a drink.

"On her deathbed, she confessed something to me that I feel the need to tell you. It just wouldn't be right if you never knew."

"Never knew what? Spit it out. I have things to do."

"It's about the boy," said the bishop.

"Ricker?" asked Sir Gregory, draining the cup and placing it back down. "What about him?"

"It seems Lady Catherine didn't want you to know."

"Know what? Tell me before I choke it out of you."

"Ricker is not your son. He is the son of Sir Jacob Quincey, my lord."

Maira gasped when she heard this. Sir Gregory looked up at the wall. She stepped back and covered the hole, hoping he hadn't heard her. She waited a few minutes and when she uncorked the hole in the wall again, the bishop was gone and in his place was the High Sheriff's right-hand man, Delbert.

"What is it, my lord?" asked Delbert.

Ricker was still in the cage but it looked as if he were sleeping.

"The Bishop of Durham has just brought to my attention that Ricker isn't my son, but instead the son of Sir Jacob Quincey."

"Ah, that is unfortunate, my lord." The guard turned and looked at Ricker in the cage. "Did you want me to do away with the lad?"

Maira bit her tongue and held her hand over her mouth. Had she just heard him correctly?"

"Nay, not the boy. I need an heir if I'm to keep Durham Castle. But I cannot take the chance that anyone knows the truth of whose son he is."

"You know you can count on me. I'll never say a word."

"I know. You are the only one I can trust. Now, what I need you to do is to get rid of the bishop."

Once again, Maira had to use all her control not to cry out.

"Shall I hang him the way I did the last bishop?"

"Nay. I am thinking a blade to the heart this time."

"I'll take care of it right away, my lord."

"Nay, you won't. We'll wait for Jacob to arrive first."

"I don't understand, High Sheriff."

"What better way to make sure I get rid of him forever? He has been a boil on my neck for too long. I want him framed again. When he shows up in his feeble attempt to attack me, kill the bishop – but with this." He tossed the jeweled dagger to the guard.

"Why this?" asked the guard.

"Because, I am going to make it known that Jacob has stolen my wife's dagger."

"I thought Lady Maira had this," said the guard, inspecting the blade.

"She did. But then she left the castle walls and returned it to Jacob."

"She did? Then why do you have it?"

"Keep up, you simpleton," said Sir Gregory, slapping the man on the side of the head. "It's the story we're using and I want it spread throughout the castle immediately. As soon as Jacob attacks, bring the bishop and kill him with the dagger and then shout out that Jacob did it."

"As you wish, my lord."

Once the guard and the High Sheriff left the room, Maira stuck the cork back into the wall and made her way to the kitchen. Slipping inside, she found Cleo and motioned for the woman to join her.

"What is it, my lady?" Cleo kept an eye on the door for the High Sheriff.

"Things are worse than we thought," explained Maira, revealing what she'd learned to the cook, wondering how she was going to proceed. So many lives were in danger and Maira wasn't sure she could protect them all. This was a horrible situation and someone was sure to die before it was all over.

CHAPTER 19

Jacob knew something was wrong the next morning when he'd approached the castle to find the wall walks void of any soldiers and the gates to the castle opened wide. It was way too easy to enter, and that concerned him. He had camped at the edge of the woods and, to his knowledge, only a dozen soldiers left on the hunt.

That wasn't right. The High Sheriff was much too greedy to only send a dozen men on the hunt. And if there were so many soldiers left in the castle, why weren't they patrolling the battlements?

He knew. The High Sheriff knew Jacob was coming. That had to be the answer. Jacob had to sneak in but, then again, mayhap Sir Gregory knew about the secret tunnels as well. This wasn't going to be easy.

Jacob knew the High Sheriff too well. Even if he did have the tunnels guarded, he wouldn't think anyone would come in through the tunnel that led into the well. Plus, the man would never want to get his hands wet. Aye, that was how Jacob was going to sneak in. Without an army, he was going to have to find the High Sheriff and kill him, and then try to appeal to the knights that used to be loyal to Jacob.

As the former Captain of the Guard, Jacob had made friends with the men he led. Hopefully, enough of them would still be loyal to him and feel the same way as the villagers about the High Sheriff. If not, he would probably lose his life in the process, but it was a chance he had to take.

Silently, he crept toward the castle and the secret tunnel under a stump that led to the well inside the courtyard. He missed Maira deeply and hoped to see her again. But even if he was killed in the process, one thought made him feel at ease. Maira was long gone from Castle Durham and hopefully by now, she and her cousin were nearly back to Whitehaven. Her father would care for them and see to their safety. Jacob would never forgive himself if anything happened to Maira. And if he died today, his biggest regret would be that he would never be able to hold her in his arms again and look into her beautiful blue eyes and tell her how much he really loved her.

* * *

"Lady Maira!"

Maira stopped in her tracks and slowly turned around. She had been carefully staying in the shadows as she sneaked to the stable, wanting to get a horse to ride out to warn Jacob. But with her ill luck, the High Sheriff saw her.

"My lord," she said, slowly turning around to see him walking across the courtyard with his sidekick, Delbert.

"I thought I locked you in your room."

"Aye, my lord, I was," she said, trying to think of an excuse. "But I snuck out when the guard left to use the garderobe."

"Delbert, did the guard at her door leave at all?" he asked his soldier.

"I don't believe so, my lord," said the man.

"Don't play me for a fool, Maira," spat the High Sheriff. "I know you snuck out through the tunnels."

"What tunnels?" she asked, hoping she sounded convincing.

"I have known about them for years. That's how my henchman, Delbert snuck out of the late bishop's room after he hung him three years ago."

"My lord! What are you telling her?" asked Delbert.

"It doesn't matter," chuckled the man. "She already knows all our plans."

"What do you mean?" she asked. Her hand wavered above her dagger.

"Don't think I don't know you were spying through the peephole."

"What peephole?"

"Shut up!" He swung at Maira but she managed to step out of the way of being hit.

"My lord, I don't think she should know all this," complained Delbert.

"It doesn't matter, you fool. Because as soon as you kill the bishop and frame Jacob, you're going to kill her, too."

"I am?"

"No one is going to do that." Maira reached behind her back and drew her sword.

"Ah, good!" The High Sheriff seemed to like the fact she'd

drawn her blade. "I would love one last swordfight with the wench. It makes my blood flow with excitement."

Maira's sword clashed with the sword of the High Sheriff. She was light on her feet and he was clunky, and that gave her the advantage. She jumped to the side as his blade swiped down next to her, ripping her gown in the process. She managed to catch him off guard and strike him across the cheek.

"Damn!" he spat, wiping the blood off his face with the back of his hand. By now, everyone crowded around to see what was happening. "I think it's time you shed a little blood as well."

The man came after her like a demon possessed, swiping his blade left and right, backing her up against the well. Then he knocked the blade from her hand and it fell into the well with a splash. He pricked the skin at the base of her neck, causing blood to drip down between her breasts. Forcefully, he reached out and grabbed her by the hair.

"Take her daggers," commanded the High Sheriff to the henchman. Delbert removed her daggers and spoke in a low voice.

"Shall I kill her now?" asked Delbert.

"Not yet," said Sir Gregory, bending over and licking the blood from between her breasts. She cringed, wanting to kill the man with her bare hands. "If she is really married to Jacob, then I want him to suffer even more by knowing that I've had her before she died."

"I'll never lay with the likes of you!" Maira dug her nails into the man's hand and pushed away from him, spitting in his eye.

He stilled with one eye closed and a smile on his face.

"Lady Maira, I want you to wash up with water from the well and then meet me in my solar."

"Why would I ever do that?" she shouted.

"Delbert, tell the guard to come forward."

"All right," shouted Delbert with a wave of his arm.

The guard who had been outside the bedchamber door walked forward holding on to Morag. Her cousin's hands were tied behind her back.

"Morag!" Maira gasped, taking a step toward her cousin, but the High Sheriff held her back.

"Nay, you don't," said the man. "You will come to me willingly to couple with me in my chamber, or my guard here will kill your cousin."

"Maira! Dinna let them kill me. Help me!" cried Morag.

Maira realized she no longer had a choice. If she didn't do as the man said, Morag would die. When she sent Morag back to the room to keep her safe, Maira had all but sealed the girl's fate. She wasn't sure if they would both be killed either way, but she couldn't do anything to help her cousin without her weapons.

"Nay, don't hurt Morag," Maira cried. "I'll come to your solar, but please let her go."

"Whether your friends live or die is up to you."

"Friends?" asked Maira, noticing he used the word in plural.

The High Sheriff motioned with his head and Maira looked up to the battlements to see Branton being held by a guard. He had his hands tied behind his back as well and had a rope around his neck that was connected to a parapet. The guard was ready to push Branton over the edge.

"God's eyes, nay!" exclaimed Maira, feeling as if this were

all her fault. And now, her cousin, her friend, and her husband would all die because she wouldn't be able to help them.

"You have five minutes," warned the High Sheriff, sheathing his sword. "If you are not in my solar by then, your friends will die either way."

"You are a heartless, no good son of a bitch," she spat.

He reached out and slapped her hard across the cheek. The force sent her sprawling against the well and she gripped the stones, feeling lightheaded and dizzy.

"Five minutes," warned the High Sheriff, walking away, leaving his henchman to watch her.

Maira wanted nothing more than to cry, but she was too furious to do it. Her blood boiled and she felt an intense hatred for the High Sheriff, wondering now why she had ever felt bad for the man when Jacob told her he was going to kill him. Sir Gregory deserved to die. And if it was the last thing she ever did, she would see to it. Aye, she would go to his solar and pretend she was there to couple with him, but she would kill him instead.

She reached down and patted her short boot to make sure the eating dagger she had hidden there this morning was still in place. It wasn't a very thick blade, but if her aim was accurate and she used enough force, she could hopefully stab it right through the man's heart and the results would be deadly.

"Lady Maira, are you coming?" called out Delbert.

She looked up to the battlements to see the guard watching over Branton. He struck up a conversation with another of the guards. Then she looked over to Morag. The guard had thrown her into the back of a wagon and was drinking from a flask.

"I'm coming," she said, following Delbert to the solar,

wondering how in Heaven's name she was going to kill the High Sheriff, save Morag and Branton, and warn Jacob all at the same time.

JACOB EMERGED from the tunnel that led from the inside of the well, almost getting hit by Maira's sword as it fell into the water from up above.

He had stayed hidden and heard what was going on, now regretting that he had dismissed his army. He didn't expect to walk into a mess like this. Having Will's help as well as the villagers he'd trained would come in handy about now. He never should have had a change of heart because someone was going to pay for it with their life.

Jacob knew Maira enough to realize she would never lay with the High Sheriff of her own accord, even if her friends' lives were in danger. Nay, she was a fighter and would never give up. He hadn't expected to find her still at the castle, but he shouldn't be surprised. Maira was not one to run from danger. But now, she had put him in a very bad position. He would have to think fast to do something to save her and her friends and still be able to kill off the High Sheriff and convince the knights and soldiers to follow him instead.

He stuck Maira's sword under his belt and grabbed on to the bucket connected to a rope, meaning to climb up. But someone started turning the handle and the bucket moved with him holding on to it. Looking up, he saw Tommy's face staring down at him.

"Hold on tightly," the boy whispered. "Alf and I will get you out of there in no time."

When he got to the top, the boys stood in front of him to block the view from the guards as he climbed out of the well.

"Lady Maira is in trouble," said Alf.

"Good thing you brought the army," added Tommy. "You'll need them."

"It's just me," mumbled Jacob, hunkering down behind the well. "Block me from the guards. I am going to the High Sheriff's chamber to help Maira."

"Are you going to kill him?" whispered Tommy.

"I'll do whatever I have to do to save my wife."

"So you really are married," said Alf. "Congratulations."

"Don't congratulate me because I'm not even sure Maira wants to be married to me."

Jacob snuck into the great hall and headed to the kitchen to access the secret tunnel. His clothes were dripping wet and he left puddles wherever he stepped.

"Sir Jacob!" Cleo saw him enter the kitchen and ran over to join him. "Are you here with the army? We are all ready to help you attack the High Sheriff and his men."

"Nay, it's just me, Cleo."

"Oh," she said making a face. "How are you going to save your son and wife and her friends all by yourself?"

"Well, I'm . . . did you say . . . son? I don't have a son."

"Aye, you do," said Cleo. "Maira told me that she heard the Bishop of Durham telling the High Sheriff that Ricker is your son. Lady Catherine confessed to him on her deathbed."

"Ricker is . . . mine?" Jacob swallowed deeply, trying to digest what he'd just heard. He liked the lad and also the idea of being a father. "Where is he?"

"Lady Maira said the High Sheriff put him in a cage in his solar."

Jacob heard that and anger and vengeance burned in his veins. "No one is going to cage my son and defile my wife. I'll kill that bastard, I swear I will." Jacob headed over to the secret tunnel.

"There's more, my lord." Cleo ran after him. "The High Sheriff is going to have his henchman kill the bishop to keep the secret of the boy not being his son. He is going to pin the murder on you again."

"Nay! I won't let that happen a second time." Jacob hurried through the tunnel, on a mission to kill the High Sheriff.

$\mathcal{M}$aira stepped into the solar trying to hold back her anger when she saw Ricker lying in the locked cage across the room. "What kind of a man are you that you would put your own son in a cage?" she asked Sir Gregory.

"Come in the room and close the door," he answered, standing at the foot of the bed.

"But I –"

"Do it!"

Ricker woke up and sat up in the cage and started crying.

"Shut up!" yelled the High Sheriff.

"You are a wretch," Maira said through gritted teeth, running to Ricker. The High Sheriff grabbed her arm and pulled her to him, staring into her eyes.

"We both know damned well he isn't mine, don't we?"

"I don't know what you mean." Maira looked the other way.

"The question is, how long will it take Jacob to find out and come after his son? And why hasn't he come for you by now? I think you lied to me when you said you were married to him."

"I didn't lie."

"Hrmph. Well, it doesn't matter either way. I'm going to have you and then I'm going to have to kill you."

"Why? You don't need to kill me."

"Oh, but how wrong you are." He reached up and stroked her chin, letting his hand linger and trail down her chest. She stood still, waiting for the opportunity to pull the knife out of her boot.

Then he smashed his lips against hers in a punishing kiss. Her instincts were to fight him, but she held back. She wanted to wait until he removed his weapons first.

"Let's get this over with, shall we?" She reached out and unbuckled his weapon belt, dropping it to the floor.

"Oooh, I like that. An aggressive woman in the bedchamber."

"Take off your clothes," she told him.

"You first." He reached out and fumbled with the laces on her gown. Wait for it, she told herself. Just hold out. But when he grabbed her breasts she could no longer hold back. She kneed him in the groin and pushed him down on the bed. She reached for his weapons, but he grabbed her and pulled her atop him. Throwing her to her back, his weight on her body kept her from reaching the blade in her boot.

"Get off of me!" she screamed, pounding her fists against his chest. At times like this, she hated being so petite. Without her weapons, she was virtually defenseless.

"Get your damned hands off my wife!" came a low, angry voice from the other side of the room.

"Jacob?" Maira turned her head to see Jacob emerging from the secret door in the wall.

"What the hell!" Sir Gregory jumped off the bed, grabbing his sword and holding it up to Jacob. "A little early aren't you, Quincey?"

"Apparently a little late, but hopefully still in time. Maira, are you all right?" he asked, his sword clashing with the High Sheriff's.

"I'm fine, Jacob. And I'm so glad to see you."

"Why didn't you go back to Whitehaven like you said you were going to do?" asked Jacob as he fought with Sir Gregory.

"I stayed to help you, Jacob. He means to frame you again by murdering the Bishop of Durham. And Ricker is your son."

"I know," said Jacob, managing to nick the High Sheriff on the hand.

"You will never get away with this," spat Sir Gregory.

"On the contrary, you are the one who won't get away with your deceitful ways."

Maira ran over and picked up the High Sheriff's dagger. "I'm going to help you, Jacob. You're not alone."

"Nay!" shouted Jacob. "Take your sword and Ricker and get out of here. Now!" He took her sword from his waist belt and threw it on the bed. She rushed over to retrieve it, putting it in the sheath attached to her back. Then she went over and got Ricker from the cage, holding him to her chest.

"Kill him, Jacob," she said. "I'll go out to the courtyard and see how your army is faring."

"Nay, Maira, there is no army."

"What did you say?" This startled her to hear this. She was counting on the villagers to help Jacob fight off the High

Sheriff's men. Jacob fought wildly against the High Sheriff as they moved around the room.

"You were right. I was only thinking of myself," Jacob admitted. "I couldn't let the villagers lose their lives for me. I let them go."

"Nay!" shouted Maira, sorry now that she had ever put the idea into his head.

"No army?" The High Sheriff laughed heartily. "This will be easier than I thought."

"Get the hell out of here and protect my son," Jacob told her.

"Aye, Jacob. I'll protect your son with my life." She ran to the door as the two men continued to fight. But she stopped on the threshold when Jacob called out to her.

"Maira."

"Aye, Jacob?" Holding Ricker tightly, she looked back over her shoulder at her husband.

"I want you to remember that whatever happens, I love you and always will."

"I love you, too," she told him, feeling the emotion welling up in her chest. She meant it. She was sure of it now, and she was sad that she had not told him sooner.

"Dada," Ricker called out, about breaking Maira's heart. She rushed out the door, pulling her sword from the sheath to protect Jacob's son, and didn't look back.

JACOB FOUGHT with the High Sheriff, and might have been able to kill him hadn't three of his guards run into the room through the open door. One of them was his seedy sidekick, Delbert, holding on to the Bishop of Durham.

"My lord," said Delbert. "You found Jacob."

"Aye," said the High Sheriff. "Get the bishop in here. We've got work to do."

"You'll not hurt the man," snapped Jacob.

"Oh, I'm not the one hurting him, but when we are done you will look like the one who killed him."

Jacob was at a disadvantage. He was wondering how he was going to fight off four men and save the bishop when he heard a sliding noise behind Sir Gregory. Glancing over the man's shoulder he saw Alf and Tommy in the secret passageway waving their arms. He quickly made his way over to the bishop, grabbed him and pushed him into the passageway, closing the door and standing in front of it with his sword raised high.

"You'll die for that," bellowed Delbert, taking a step toward him.

"Wait," said the High Sheriff. "I have a better idea."

CHAPTER 21

Maira rushed to the kitchen with Ricker in her arms, happy to find Cleo and all of the servants waiting for her. Most of them had items in their hands that could be used as weapons, whether it be a broom, a poker from the fire, or even just pots and pans.

"I've rounded up the servants and we're all here to help Jacob," Cleo announced.

"Good, because he dismissed his army and he'll have no other help," said Maira feeling horrible now. "Cleo, it's my fault he has no army and that he is probably going to die trying to protect me."

"He's not going to die," said Cleo in a firm and scolding voice. "Maira, you need to stay strong."

"But I can't fight as good as a man. I don't have the physical strength. I know that now."

"Then look inside yourself and find strength there instead. You are a Follower of the Secret Heart, Maira. Do I have to remind you of that?"

"Nay, I know. But I don't know what to do."

"The queen had faith that one day you would do wondrous things. She had faith in you and now you need to have faith in yourself. Don't let her down. Don't let any of us down. We are all counting on you. Especially Jacob, whether he admits it or not."

"You're right," said Maira with a determined nod. "Now, the first thing I need to do is to save Morag and Branton."

"There you go," said Cleo just as the secret door opened and out ran Alf and Tommy, along with the Bishop of Durham.

"What's going on?" asked the very confused bishop.

"Bishop," said Maira. "The High Sheriff wants you dead and he is planning on framing Jacob just like he did three years ago with the death of the Bishop of Somerset."

"Oh, I see," said the bishop. "What can I do to help?"

"Cleo," said Maira. "Go with Tommy, Alf and the bishop. Take Ricker as well and get to the stable. Get in a wagon and ride out of here as fast as you can."

"But what about you?" asked Cleo.

"I'm staying to help my friends as well as to help Jacob."

"I'll do what you say but I don't like the idea of leaving you behind."

"It's more important that you protect the bishop and the children," said Maira. "Take the tunnels and you should be able to sneak out to the stable. I will go out to the courtyard and try to make a distraction."

"Be careful, Maira," warned Cleo. "We would hate to lose you. You're the best thing this castle has ever had and I'd like to see that continue."

"With any luck, you'll see not only me but also Jacob bringing Durham Castle back to what it used to be."

Maira first made her way up the battlements, knowing she could use the help of Branton since he was good with a blade. She hid in the shadows and waited until there was only one guard standing with Branton, getting ready for the High Sheriff's word to throw the boy off the battlements. Then when the guard walked over to take a piss over the side wall, she snuck up behind Branton.

He saw her and turned his head. She put a finger to her lips to warn him to be quiet. Then she used her blade to cut the ropes that bound his hands and feet. Branton quickly took the noose off from over his head.

The guard looked over his shoulder, and Branton rushed him, knocking him over the wall into the moat and taking his sword that was resting against the wall.

"Good work," said Maira.

Branton's eyes opened wide. "Look out behind you."

Maira turned to see another guard with his sword raised, about to plunge it into her back. Branton knocked her down and jumped over her and thrust his sword into the man's chest. The guard fell over the battlements into the courtyard.

"You killed a man to save me," said Maira in shock, not expecting this at all.

"I know. It's the first man I've actually killed and I'd do it again if I had to in order to save someone who means so much to me," Branton told her.

"Then you might get your chance. There is a guard holding Morag in the courtyard. We need to save her next."

"Let's go," said Branton, leading the way.

When the guard fell from the battlements into the courtyard, it caused the distraction needed. Maira saw Cleo driving the wagon over the drawbridge with the bishop holding

Ricker in the back. Tommy and Alf rode out of the stable on horses and headed toward her.

"Morag," said Maira as they approached her. Branton fought with the guard while Maira cut her ropes.

"Maira, I'm so frightened. We're all goin' to die," cried Morag.

"Nay, you won't. Be strong, Morag."

"Maira, we've got horses," called out Alf as the boys approached. "Get on, quickly."

Maira helped Morag atop the horse with Alf, but she did not join them. "Branton, go with them to protect them," said Maira.

"Nay, I won't leave you," protested the boy, taking down another man. Branton was proving to be a loyal warrior.

"Do it. It is an order," she shouted. "I need someone who can protect them and it has to be you."

"What about you, Maira?" asked Branton. "Who will protect you?"

"I'll take to the tunnels and go back to help Jacob. Now please, I don't want to have to worry about Morag and the boys."

"I'll protect them, Maira. You can count on me." Branton jumped atop the horse with Tommy and they all managed to leave the castle just as the High Sheriff came out of the keep. Behind him was Delbert holding a blade to Jacob's throat. Jacob was bruised and bleeding and could barely stand.

"Jacob!" cried Maira, rushing toward him with her sword drawn.

"Take a step closer and I'll kill him," shouted Delbert. Maira noticed Jacob's hands were tied behind him and that he could barely walk. By the angle of one of his legs it almost looked as if it were broken.

"Nay, don't hurt him," she begged. "Please."

"Fight me, wench," said the High Sheriff. "It turns me on."

"What?" she asked, backing away as he drew his sword.

"Leave her alone, it's me you want," Jacob shouted.

"Nay," snarled the High Sheriff. "You'll watch us fight and then you'll witness me taking the wench right here in the courtyard in front of everyone. That will prove she is my wife and not yours."

"You bastard!" Jacob broke away from Delbert but as soon as he did, Delbert hit him over the head with the hilt of his sword. Jacob fell to the ground, shaking his head as if he were dazed.

"Don't kill him yet, you fool. I want him to suffer first," snapped the High Sheriff.

Maira had no choice but to fight with the High Sheriff. He toyed with her at first, and then started coming after her with his blade with a vengeance.

She fought her best, but the man was crazed and, soon, her sword was flung from her hand and he pushed her to the ground.

"Now, it's time for a little fun," said the High Sheriff, untying his breeches and straddling her. Maira fought against him but he held her down with his body and one beefy hand.

"Leave her alone," screamed Jacob.

Maira heard the snap of ropes and a scuffle and then the sound of a body hitting the ground. Jacob somehow managed to kill Delbert and pick up his sword. He charged the High Sheriff, limping on his hurt leg.

"Get him, you fools," shouted the High Sheriff, sending a dozen guards toward Jacob. "Kill him."

"Nay," Maira cried, digging her nails into the man, but his arms were covered in leather and it didn't do much to deter him.

Just when Maira thought it was the end for her and Jacob, she heard shouting and looked over to see the servants of the castle run out of the keep. They started fighting with their makeshift weapons.

The next sound came from the front gate.

"Charge," came a shout that sounded like Will. He rode through the gates with the villagers following. They all had their weapons and burst into the courtyard fighting against Sir Gregory's soldiers. She even saw Jacob's brother, Father Frank, with a rake in his hand.

Maira's heart soared. Jacob's army, as well as the servants, had come to his aid. She kneed the High Sheriff in the groin and managed to roll out from under him. She picked up her sword and started to fight with his soldiers to help the villagers.

JACOB MANAGED to break out from the soldiers holding him, trying to ignore the pain of his leg as he picked up a sword in each hand and limped over toward Sir Gregory.

"No one is going to take what is mine," he growled. "And no one is going to touch my wife and live to tell about it."

The High Sheriff got up and grabbed his sword but it was too late. Jacob's vengeance would finally be served. He took the man down and stuck both the swords through the High Sheriff's heart. Then he looked up and shouted loudly.

"Stop the fighting," he called out. "The High Sheriff is dead. I won't have the deaths of innocent people on my head. Those knights and soldiers who will pay allegiance to me, drop your swords and get down on one knee. For those who still follow Sir Gregory, I will give you one minute to get the hell out of here and never return."

There were some men who hightailed it out of the courtyard, but most of the soldiers vowed to honor Jacob and got down on one knee.

"Jacob!" Maira dropped her sword and ran to him. He gathered her in his arms and kissed her over and over again.

"Maira, I don't ever want anything to come between us again."

"And neither will it," she said.

"Where is my son?" Jacob scanned the courtyard.

"There's the boy," someone yelled. He turned to see Cleo driving a horse and wagon into the courtyard. The Bishop of Durham was in the back with Ricker cradled safely on his lap. Behind them rode Alf and Morag and Branton and Tommy. They all came to join him.

"Ricker," shouted Jacob, reaching over and taking the boy from the bishop. "Come here, Son." He held the little boy to his chest and kissed him, keeping one arm around Maira at the same time. He was never going to let go of what was his again.

"Someone else approaches," shouted one of the soldiers.

"Maira, I think it's your father if I'm not mistaken," Jacob told her.

.   .   .

Maira looked up to see her father riding through the gate with a small army of men.

"Father," she cried, running to him.

Rowen, her father, dismounted and gathered her into his arms.

"Maira, I'm sorry I sent you here. As soon as I realized it was a mistake, I came right away. I only hope I'm not too late."

"Father, the High Sheriff was a horrible man and framed Sir Jacob for killing a bishop three years ago."

"Sir Jacob?"

"Father, I'd like you to meet Sir Jacob Quincey. My husband."

"Your . . . husband?" Rowen cocked his head and studied Jacob. "I don't understand."

"We're married," Maira told him. "Jacob is the man I chose to wed."

"All right." Rowen nodded, looking at the dead bodies of the High Sheriff, Delbert, and about a dozen others. "What the hell happened here?"

"My lord, if I may," said Jacob, holding on to Ricker, limping over to them. "I would like to explain everything to you. But first I want to say I am in love with your daughter, Maira, and would like your permission to marry her."

"But I thought you were already married," said Rowen.

"We are, but I would like your blessing."

"This is the man you want as your husband, Maira?" asked Rowen.

"He is, Father. I love him."

"But hasn't he been excommunicated not to mention stripped of his title if I'm not mistaken?"

"It was all a mistake," said Jacob.

"I can vouch for that," said the Bishop of Durham getting out of the cart. "The High Sheriff tried to kill me and Sir Jacob saved my life. Sir Gregory was also responsible for killing the Bishop of Somerset. I will personally talk to the pope and make sure that Jacob's excommunication is reversed and that his title is restored."

"Would you really do that for me?" asked Jacob with a large smile.

"I've seen some remarkable things here today," said the bishop. "If all these villagers as well as the servants, including women and children, would risk their lives to come to your aid, then I am sure you will be not only Lord of Durham, but you will be granted the title of High Sheriff as well."

"I would like that," said Jacob softly, pulling Maira to him and kissing her atop the head.

"Dada, I like, too," said Ricker, making everyone laugh.

CHAPTER 22

THREE WEEKS LATER

"*M*aira, they're here! Hurry!" called out Morag, rushing down from the battlements of Durham Castle holding up the hem of her gown.

"Morag, be careful or you're going to hurt yourself." Maira walked across the courtyard to meet her.

"Ye are too protective, Maira." Morag pushed past her and ran to the gate, waiting for the small entourage to enter. Maira expected her mother and father but she didn't know her cousin, Willow, and Willow's new husband, Conrad, would be with them. Her mouth fell open when she saw her cousin, Fia, with her husband, Alastair, and their new baby girl, Oletha, as well.

"Fia!" cried Morag, running across the drawbridge to greet her sister. Maira ran after her to meet them as well. They were all escorted by Maira's father, Rowen, who had gone back to get the rest of the family. Maira's uncles, Rook and Reed, were with them.

"Mother," called out Maira excitedly, hopping up onto the wagon to hug her mother, Cordelia. Maira's youngest brother, Michael, was there as well and Maira reached over and hugged him and kissed him on his cheek.

"Maira, stop that," complained Michael, making a face and wiping off his cheek with the back of his hand.

"Maira, I must say I like seeing this side of you," laughed Cordelia. "You are more like a lady and less like a warrior with all this kissing and hugging."

"Our daughter will always be a warrior," stated Rowen, riding up on a horse next to the wagon that was being driven by a servant.

"Father, she's not a warrior, she's only a girl," said Maira's ten-year-old brother. "But I'm going to be a mighty warrior someday, just like you."

"Where are William, Philip, and Theodore?" asked Maira, hoping to see the rest of her brothers. "I had hoped they'd be here, too."

"Now Maira, you know your brothers are being fostered. I'm sorry but they couldn't make it," said Cordelia.

"William is training for knighthood in a few years," said Rowen proudly. "And Philip and Theodore have just been made squires."

"How exciting," said Maira, glancing across the courtyard to see Branton and Jacob heading in their direction. Jacob's leg was still in a splint, but he was able to walk much better now.

"Welcome," shouted Jacob, waving a hand over his head.

"Is that your husband?" asked Maira's mother, stretching her neck to see him. "He's very handsome."

"Aye, he is." Maira helped her mother off the cart. "Mother, I would like you to meet my husband, Jacob."

"Sir Jacob Quincey at your service," said Jacob, kissing Maira's mother on the back of her hand.

"Did you say, Sir?" asked Rowen, dismounting.

"Aye, Father," Maira explained. "With word from the Bishop of Durham and also the help of Jacob's brother, Father Frank, the pope has reversed the excommunication and Jacob has been cleared of the false charges."

"That's wonderful," said Rowen, shaking Jacob's hand. "Congratulations."

"I've also reclaimed my title," explained Jacob.

"That's right," said Maira, slipping her arm around Jacob's waist. He pulled her closer in a hug. "Jacob is once again Sir Jacob and not only the new Lord of Durham Castle but also the new High Sheriff."

"And I'm his new squire," said Branton proudly.

"That's right," said Will. "And I've been knighted, so Branton will take my place."

"So you're a squire at last. It's about time." Willow sauntered over with Conrad to greet everyone. Fia and Morag walked over arm in arm and Fia's husband, Conrad, approached holding their baby daughter.

"Sir Jacob has given me a new sword," said Branton proudly, holding it in the air to show them.

"Dinna point that thing at me or my family or ye'll find yer head severed and lyin' on the ground," warned Alastair, still sore since Branton had tried to kill him at one time.

"I'm sorry about that. It won't happen again," said Branton, quickly lowering the sword and slinking away to the back of the crowd.

"So, I hear ye are already married," said Fia, greeting Maira with a hug.

"Aye, and you are all just in time for the celebration," Morag broke in. "We have the great hall decorated and Cleo has cooked up somethin' special. Haggis!"

They all laughed.

"Who is Cleo?" asked Willow.

"She's not only a cook but someone very special," said Maira, planning to tell the girls later that Cleo was also a Follower of the Secret Heart. "Here she comes now with her son as well as Jacob's son, Ricker."

Cleo approached, holding the little boy's hand. Tommy was right next to her, smiling from ear to ear, wearing a pair of his new shoes. Maira had kept her promise to Tommy, giving him not one but three new pairs of shoes. The servants and villagers were also happy since Jacob was the new lord and cared for them well.

Maira scooped up Ricker from Cleo's arms and kissed him on the cheek. "Mama," said Ricker.

"Mama?" Willow asked, exchanging glances with Fia. "So you are already a mother."

"She's goin' to be a mother again soon," blurted out Morag.

"You are?" asked Jacob.

"Morag, you can't keep a secret," spat Maira. "I haven't even told Jacob yet that I'm pregnant."

"We're going to have a baby?" Jacob whooped aloud and pulled Maira and Ricker to him in a hug.

"She's no' the only one havin' a baby," said Morag.

"Morag, I just told you that information. I wanted to be the one to tell Maira," complained Willow.

"You are pregnant, too?" asked Maira. "This is wonderful. All the cousins are going to be mothers."

"No' all of us," said Morag, sulking.

"You'll have your time, too," Maira assured her. "You don't need to feel left out."

"The food is ready if anyone is hungry," said Cleo.

"What is that brooch you're wearing?" Willow asked her.

Cleo's hand covered the heart brooch and she looked over to Maira.

"It's all right, Cleo. There is no need to keep it a secret. I was going to tell my cousins later and I've already told Jacob about the Followers of the Secret Heart. Willow and Fia, Cleo is a member as well."

The girls were surprised and walked over to meet Cleo.

"It's snowing," called out Michael, opening his mouth to the sky, trying to catch snowflakes on his tongue.

"Did I hear somethin' about haggis?" Reed, the red-haired triplet, came forward with his dark-haired brother, Rook.

"I say we all get out of the cold and get something to eat," stated Rook. "I'm starved."

"I hope someone brought some Mountain Magic," said Reed, talking about the potent whisky that was brewed by the old Scot, Callum MacKeefe.

"Faither, now that my cousins are married, do I still have to stay in Rothbury?" asked Morag. "With Branton a squire for Sir Jacob, if I go back, I'll be all alone."

"That's true," said Rowen. "But when the earl left to campaign for the king, he told me he didn't want to be guardian anymore."

"Then ye'll come home to Scotland with me, Morag," said Reed. "Yer mathair will be happy to have ye home."

"Ye can help me with the baby," said Fia.

"Everyone is married and havin' babies but me," scoffed Morag. "When will I have a turn? I am always forgotten."

"Mayhap, if ye'd stop spillin' everyone's secrets, a laddie might want ye someday," said Reed.

"I dinna think anyone will ever want me," pouted Morag.

"That's not true," said Maira. "There is always a chance. After all, I never thought I'd marry and, yet, here I am."

"Wife, I've been meaning to give you this," said Jacob, pulling the jeweled dagger from his waist belt and holding it out to Maira. Maira put Ricker on the ground and took the dagger with both hands.

"But Jacob, this is the dagger that used to be your mother's. I know how much it means to you."

"Isna that the dagger he gave his last lover?" asked Morag. "Ye ken who I mean. Lady Catherine. Ricker's mathair who is dead."

"Morag, haud yer wheesht," said Fia under her breath.

"And you wonder why no man wants you? How insensitive of you to say that," grumbled Willow in her normal haughty manner.

"I'm sorry," said Morag, looking to the ground. She seemed as if she were going to cry.

"It's all right, Morag," said Maira giving her a half-hug. "I don't let things of the past bother me. And I am honored that Jacob loves me enough to give this to me. Thank you, Husband. I will cherish it always." She tucked the dagger into her waist belt, loving the weapon. "However, now that I'm Lady of the Castle and soon to be the mother of two, I think my warrior ways are going to be reserved only for protecting my family and those in my care."

"I appreciate that," said Jacob, pulling her to him and kissing hcr passionately in front of everyone. "And I also appreciate the fact that you told me your secret of being a Follower of the Secret Heart. However, I don't ever want you to stop being who you are. As a matter of fact, I think my new squire is going to need all the practice he can get. Mayhap, you can keep him in line for me."

"Branton will make a wonderful squire and doesn't need my help," said Maira, throwing the boy a smile. "And I promise to always be open and honest with you, Jacob. With you as my husband and at my side, I know I will no longer hold any *Rebellious Secrets.*"

FROM THE AUTHOR

I hope you enjoyed Maira and Jacob's story and, if so, that you will take the time to leave a review for me.

While Maira was more physical than her cousins, Willow and Fia, she also felt as if she had to protect everyone. But sometimes that comes at a price, like when she put herself in danger's way, not worrying about protecting herself. But then again, as a mother I know this feeling that Maira had. All fear is pushed aside to protect those we love.

Be sure to read the next book in the series, Forgotten Secrets – Book 4. And if you've missed Fia or Willow's stories, you'll want to pick up the first two books, Highland Secrets – Book 1, and Seductive Secrets – Book 2. Also available in print and audiobook format.

Thanks to everyone for all your support. It means the world to me. You are the reason I write!

Elizabeth Rose

ABOUT ELIZABETH

Elizabeth Rose is a multi-published, bestselling author, writing medieval, historical, contemporary, paranormal, and western romance. Her books are available as EBooks, paperbacks, and audiobooks as well.

Her favorite characters in her works include dark, dangerous and tortured heroes, and feisty, independent heroines who know how to wield a sword. She loves writing 14th century medieval novels, and is well-known for her many series.

Her twelve-book small town contemporary series, Tarnished Saints, was inspired by incidents in her own life.

After being traditionally published, she started self-publishing, creating her own covers and book trailers on a dare from her two sons.

Elizabeth loves the outdoors. In the summertime, you can find her in her secret garden with her laptop, swinging in her hammock working on her next book. Elizabeth is a born storyteller and passionate about sharing her works with her readers.

Please visit her website at **Elizabethrosenovels.com** to read excerpts from any of her novels and get sneak peeks at covers of upcoming books. You can follow her on **Twitter, Facebook, Goodreads** or **BookBub.** Be sure to sign up for her

newsletter so you don't miss out on new releases or upcoming events.

ALSO BY ELIZABETH ROSE

Medieval

Legendary Bastards of the Crown Series

Seasons of Fortitude Series

Secrets of the Heart Series

Legacy of the Blade Series

Daughters of the Dagger Series

MadMan MacKeefe Series

Barons of the Cinque Ports Series

Second in Command Series

Holiday Knights Series

Highland Chronicles Series

Medieval/Paranormal

Elemental Magick Series

Greek Myth Fantasy Series

Tangled Tales Series

Contemporary

Tarnished Saints Series

Working Man Series

Western

Cowboys of the Old West Series

And more!

Please visit http://elizabethrosenovels.com

Elizabeth Rose

Made in the USA
Middletown, DE
28 September 2021

49264065R00149